DEEP PERIL

~~~~~~~~~~~~~

DEEP PERIL

~~~~~~~~~~~~~

Scott Slocum

ISBN-13: 978-1-960583-96-3 print edition

ISBN-13: 978-1-960583-97-0 e-book edition

Waterside Productions
2055 Oxford Ave, Cardiff, CA 92007
www.waterside.com

Dedication

~~~~~~~~~~~~~~~~~~~~~~~~~~

For Carol, who has supported me in every endeavor I have attempted over more than 50 years of marriage.

Beginning Play

~~~~~~~~~~~~~~~~

When his cell phone rang he grabbed it quickly and uttered one word: "Yes?"

"Okay, it's a deal. You can begin. The down payment has been deposited in the account you specified. The rest will follow when the job is done."

"I've already been at this three days – I know exactly what to do. Our formal engagement will begin when I have payment confirmation from the bank."

He hung up the phone without uttering another word. On the other end of the line, Gregory Salinas looked blankly at his assistant.

"Well, Mr. Salinas," the assistant asked, "did he accept, is this a go?"

Gregory's face looked suddenly ashen. He was in a drastic business situation, but he was still having second thoughts about what he'd just put into motion. His research-vessel company, Ocean Surveyors, was in serious trouble. Every major project contract in the past two years had been won by his competitor, Frontier Explorers. This phone call was a last, admittedly desperate attempt to level the playing field, balance the equation and win the next round. The stakes couldn't be higher. Extreme times do call for extreme measures.

"Mr. Salinas?" Greg's assistant asked again.

"Oh. Yes. It's a go – contingent on proof that the money has reached his bank."

"I made the transfer myself. Two hundred fifty thousand dollars, the rest of the million to follow. He has a secret escrow account. I certainly hope he's worth it."

Salinas damn well hoped so too. Convinced that his company's entire survival was at stake, his decision to hire the gentleman in question had been the last step down a very slippery slope. Salinas had already made a series of efforts to undermine his competitor's research this summer aboard the *Aladdin*, but each ploy had failed. Hiring this very expensive but perfectly positioned saboteur was Salinas' final thrust. The gentleman, with his current deviant passion for crime and money, had promised to go in and put an end to the entire project – as long as Salinas didn't ask any questions.

The gentleman checked his watch. He had a plane west to catch in order to set up his next move. He would check with the bank later on, but he knew that Salinas wouldn't be foolish enough to try to game him. He smiled for the first time that day. Yes, Salinas was a wimp when it came to really accomplishing something, but the money was quite adequate. Furthermore, there was the lingering issue of overdue revenge and the satisfying challenge of returning to a professional world he'd fairly recently been a part of. Yes, this should prove quite stimulating.

Salinas had informed him that three others had already attempted to sabotage the ship and sink the research – but they had been rank amateurs and overly squeamish about doing what was required. He on the other hand was worth his asking price because there was nothing he would not do. And he already knew who his initial touch would be, his ticket to ride. Game on.

A stand-in man had recently been transferred by Frontier Explorers to join the research vessel *Aladdin* in San Diego, replacing a critical member of the crew who had been a victim of a hit-and-run. Having just finished up an important project off Greenland and recently divorced, he was available for the assignment.

He hurried to catch a flight out of St. John's, Newfoundland, for a series of connections to San Diego. He hated flying and he hated long trips, and by the time he arrived, all he wanted was a hotel, a shower, and a bed. Proceeding to baggage claim, he encountered a man about his age, dressed in a dark suit and a chauffeur's cap, holding a sign with his name on it. He raised his hand and the chauffeur approached him. They were about the same size, but the chauffeur was full-bearded and wearing mirrored sunglasses and a leather jacket.

"I'm Greenway, sir. I've been instructed by your employer to transport you to your hotel. Tomorrow I'll take you to your ship."

"Oh, good, thank you."

He waited for his duffel bag and steel briefcase to emerge while the fellow called Greenway went to fetch the car. "Get comfortable in the back seat," Greenway offered in a rather gruff tone. "The ride to your hotel will take us about forty minutes."

He was not familiar with the area, so he did not at first find it odd that they appeared to be moving away from the city lights and onto secondary roads. He assumed that his employer had found a resort hotel out of town, but it didn't make much sense to head away from the port area rather than staying in a location near the harbor. Something felt not quite right, but he was exhausted. It had been a very long day. He was likely overreacting.

But just to test Greenway he asked, "Do you know at what time the ship departs tomorrow?"

Greenway's still-mirrored eyes shifted to the rearview mirror to observe his passenger. "Two forty-five sharp." The tone was matter-of-fact with no warmth in it. "We've got plenty of time to get there, don't worry. I'm scheduled to pick you up at ten-fifteen."

Very convenient, but the atmosphere in the car now felt overtly chilling. Greenway was a strange man. He moved his hand to the car door and explored the handle with his fingers. The handle didn't move. He wrapped his hand around the latch and pulled harder. It was locked.

"It won't open – safety function. Now just sit back and relax."

The sudden informality plus the overly-officious tone of the driver – not to mention the locked door – unsettled him. He'd been watching a kidnapping movie on the plane and he suddenly felt a twinge of fear. Was he being abducted? After all, no one had told him that he would be met by a chauffeur at the airport.

His mind started racing as he vaguely considered his options – just sit tight and stop worrying, make a phone call and check on the chauffeur, or do something like in the movie – prepare to lunge at the driver the next time the car stopped and force him to release the passenger door so he could make his escape.

He reached for his phone, but just then the car swerved sharply and skidded to a halt on the shoulder. He was thrown all over the back seat, and before he could recover, the driver was out of the car and opening the side door.

"Drop the phone," he ordered.

"What's going on here?"

And that was when he saw the small black pistol.

Aboard *Aladdin* preparations were complete for getting underway. The crew had moved aboard; the ship had been refueled; and all stores were loaded. The research team was still ashore except for Dr. Aaron Kline, the

Senior Scientist, who simply wanted to avoid another night in another hotel, and Jason Crocker, a recent PhD graduate, who wanted more time to explore the ship before things got busy.

It was also an opportunity for Jason to let his uncle know that he had arrived. Scranton Hennessy, a US Senator in his late fifties, was an advocate for getting the United States to sign the United Nations Law of the Sea treaty and thereby to acknowledge the International Seabed Authority and its responsibilities for establishing rules for deep sea mining. The majority of his Senate colleagues disagreed, unwilling to cede any control to the UN – a deal-breaker.

In addition to the career opportunities inherent in conducting research with some of the biggest reputations in the business, Jason had accepted his mission to observe the work with Frontier Explorers supporting Dr. Kline and his team, who were looking for ways to mine the ocean floor with and without causing ecological damage.

"Uncle Scranton, I made it to San Diego, and I'm aboard *Aladdin*. From what I can tell, this is a polished outfit. The ship is in great shape, and the people I've met so far are taking their work seriously. So seriously, in fact, that this will be my last call. We have to turn in our cell phones."

The Senator responded with well wishes for Jason's research and a reminder that when the cruise was over he wanted a full report.

- 2 -
Preparations for Sea
~~~~~~~~~~~~~~~~

Karen had become seriously enthralled by Professor Gordon Blake and the excitement of deep-sea exploration during the Intro lecture for the course he gave at UC San Diego Scripps Institution of Oceanography that semester. The auditorium was small, well lit, and modern. A large screen dominated the wall behind the podium. Professor Blake, a thin greying man in his late fifties, had entered the room quickly and mounted the platform with a spring in his step, grasping the sides of the lectern with a gesture of enthusiasm.

"Good morning. I'm Professor Gordon Blake," he began. "Not to put too fine a point on it, I am convinced that you'll find this elective the most important course you take while pursuing your master's degree." He stopped to measure his audience. His eyes passed over Karen, then returned to her – she looked so enthusiastic.

"Some of you are preparing for research careers, others plan to teach. Those are commendable goals, to be sure – but I hope to recruit some of you for field study in pursuit of what I consider the truly unknown. Water covers over 70 percent of the Earth's surface. And now that we know there is life at every level of the world's oceans, we need to abandon two-dimensional thinking. Virtually all of the Earth's habitable environment is water – and about three-quarters of that is deep ocean."

Karen had been hooked already by his words, even before he turned off the lights in preparation for some visuals. The lectern bulb made eerie shadows on his face, and highlighted his bushy eyebrows. "If one were to visit Earth in search of the dominant life form, what would it be?" he went on. "I suspect some of you would say humans, or insects because there are so many of them – or perhaps trees, as they cover vast expanses of the Earth's surface."

He switched on the projector and filled the screen with strange glowing translucent creatures from the ocean depths. The audience gaped at long undulating snakes, large spiny fish with long needle-like teeth, and schools of lesser denizens of the deep with similar alien characteristics. "These, ladies and gentlemen, are in fact the life forms that dominate the Earth."

After a short pause he continued, "Ancient man feared the abyss. The ocean was filled with large, hostile monsters that emerged from unknown depths to strangle ships and swallow men (and to be politically correct, they swallowed women, too, I suppose). Today we know that the sea abounds with life to the deepest reaches we have explored – and hot sulfuric vents many thousands of feet below the surface are teeming with undocumented life forms. Marine life thrives under pressure and in temperature extremes that until recently kept mankind at bay. But right now, at this very moment, we are preparing to go down and explore vast realms of earthly life never before seen – not to mention remarkable treasures of precious minerals that will transform human society.

"The ocean floor is our new frontier. Given the sheer volume of water that covers the surface of our planet, we have done minimal exploring. Unlike space with its vast reaches open to exploration by the human eye and telescopes, the dark ocean denies us access. Light fades after a few hundred feet, murk defeats our efforts to light our way below, and pressure at depth can crush us – but the rewards will be beyond imagination.

"The ocean floor is rich with minerals that are critical for our battery-powered twenty-first-century lives: our cell phones, electric vehicles, super computers. How we mine them is also critical. Done recklessly, the ecological damage would be capable of destroying the world's oceans. There is so much we don't know."

And on and on he went, with Karen soaking up every statistic, mesmerized by the images swimming in her mind. And right then the thought occurred to her that she would give anything, anything at all, to be involved in Deep Ocean research, even at the risk of her life. She felt so totally at home with this group of around fifty students eagerly taking in the famous professor's every word.

As the lecture came to an end, Karen rose with the rest of the students. Glancing casually around, she noticed a particular young man looking right back into her eyes from about thirty feet away. Did she know him from some class? No – complete stranger, although quite a handsome stranger, around her height, five foot ten, with sandy blond hair.

But, why that intense focused look on his face? She felt slightly spooked by his fixation on her, and turned to walk quickly out of the lecture hall. He followed her as she pushed through the revolving door into the bright afternoon sunlight of early spring. She headed for the bus stand.

He came right up behind her without her noticing him. "Karen! Karen, wait!"

She jumped, not recognizing the youthful male voice. Although she'd been pursuing her master's degree at the Scripps Institution since September, she didn't know many of her classmates. She stopped, turned around and found herself facing that same lanky blond male she'd seen in the lecture hall.

"Hi," he said a bit bashfully. "I was just wondering what you thought of the old man's performance?"

The question was unexpected and the derogatory reference to Professor Blake's 'performance' offended her.

"Who are you? Do I know you?" she demanded. "And why did you call Professor Blake's lecture a performance?"

"I know Gordon. He loves his work but he also loves to dazzle. He was trying hard just now to impress you with the extent of his knowledge and the limits of yours. Don't get me wrong, the guy is rock-solid. His scholarship is world-renowned, and underneath that giant ego is a mostly kind, almost gentle man."

"How do you know so much about him?"

"I'm researching Deep Ocean microbiology."

"Oh, so how do you know my name?"

"I've seen you around campus. You're attractive. So yeah, I looked up your photo and name in grad-student records. I hope that's not a sin."

"What! You're actually stalking me?"

"I saw you go into the professor's lecture so I followed you in. Is that stalking? I don't think it's a crime for a guy to be attracted to a girl. Besides, to be honest, you were attending the same Intro lecture on The Deep Sea that got me hooked a few years back."

Karen looked for the first time deeply into his eyes. He grinned in a very friendly way. "So – I don't bite. How about we catch coffee or something, talk about our burgeoning careers diving for all those vast riches of the deep?"

She felt torn. He was attractive, but the first big love affair of her life, which had felt like forever and ever, had ended tragically. She now found herself repulsed by the very idea of someone new. She saw her transportation approaching. The next bus wouldn't be along for another thirty minutes. She raised her hand as if in self-defense.

"Thanks for the offer but I've got a bus to catch. Nice talking to you. Later maybe. Gotta go."

She started to trot off to the arriving bus, her brunette hair waving behind her like a flag unfurling in retreat. He ran after her. "Can I at least have your number and call you?"

She shouted across the widening gap between them, "Sorry – gotta go."

It was not until she settled in her seat on the bus that she realized she'd been so defensive she never even got his name – and that was too bad. He had such nice eyes under that unruly shock of hair. What a curious encounter.

And that encounter brought back memories long buried. Her high school experience with boys was a series of relationships with shallow young men who did not see her for who she was. Her dim view of teenage boys did not change until she met Tim. Halfway through her Junior year in Florida, she attended an ecology class with him. They shared a love of marine life that ultimately found them on scuba-diving dates. By spring of Senior year, they were an item. But Tim was reckless. In May of that year, he dove to explore a sunken wreck and got tangled in the hull. By the time rescuers located him, he had drowned.

For days after that, Karen had felt unusually lonely, and while walking from one class to the next she looked hopefully for the young man with the bright blue eyes – but she never encountered him. She did, however, take the Professor's course, and when he offered a summer internship on board a research vessel in the Pacific, she arranged a meeting with him to discuss the offer.

On an unusually warm early-summer day they got together at a street café for a one-on-one discussion. She arrived early but Blake was already there, engrossed in some article he had brought with him. Karen hesitated to interrupt him and stopped several paces from the table, examining her potential mentor. The Professor's face was heavily lined, making him appear older than he actually was – and in his concentration he looked severe. However, when he looked up and saw her, he had a ready smile and laughing blue eyes which gave him a boyish look.

After some small talk and once they had ordered, he got down to business: "Karen, I've noted your excellent work in my course – very well done. You have what it takes, and I'm pleased you're interested in my summer internship."

She smiled back, still unsure about devoting her summer to an ocean cruise; she was also highly interested in several oceanography themes besides exploring the deep sea. "You seemed rather vague," she put in, "when you mentioned the internship during your lecture."

"Yes. And of necessity I must ask you not to talk with anyone about what I'm going to tell you today, whether or not you embark for the research."

He looked quite serious. She nodded in agreement. "Okay. I won't," she said.

"We'll be aboard quite a large private research vessel named *Aladdin*. Interning with me this summer could be one of your career's most important decisions. The research is not trivial – in fact just the opposite. We're on the brink of some major new deep-sea discoveries.

"We are out to learn more about specific places on the ocean floor where indigenous life forms feed quite happily on toxic chemicals and survive in water hot enough to melt lead." He paused a moment, sipped his coffee. "But there's more. Do you remember me telling my class about deep-sea rewards beyond imagination, just waiting to be found and mined?"

"Yes, and I'm up to date on the controversies surrounding deep-sea mining." To make her point, she added, "With immeasurable quantities of rare minerals up for grabs, obviously there's going to be a scramble at high corporate levels to dominate that new gold rush – cobalt, nickel, manganese and so forth scattered on the sea floor. Nodules the size of potatoes covering millions of acres – millions of tons."

"Yes," he nodded, "and to harvest those nodules, mining companies intend to rather savagely scrape great swathes of virgin sea floor, devastating everything down there, stirring up giant toxic clouds that will suffocate life throughout the oceans."

"But I also read," Karen went on, proud of her knowledge, "that the United Nations set up something called the 'Convention on the Law of the Sea' back in the 1980s, if I remember correctly, allocating about fifty million square miles to individual nations as Exclusive Economic Zones off their shores – and about the same total area to what I think they called an economic common heritage of mankind."

"So you *have* studied this," he said, quite pleased.

She grinned. "Yeah. I wrote a quick paper on it."

"And how do you stand in regard to deep-sea mining" he queried, watching her response closely. "We do very much need those minerals for batteries."

She frowned at him. "Oh, I don't know! The minerals *are* badly needed, but we have to be very careful not to wreck the ecology down there. That could be the final nail in our world coffin. You must know that."

He leaned back in his chair, eyed her for a moment. "Karen, why would you actually think I would be in favor of that?"

"Well I would hope not," she retorted rather hotly. "Otherwise I'm not at all interested in your internship."

"Well, and again mum's the word, I'm sharing *Aladdin's* charter with Dr. Aaron Kline. I and my research team are embarking to study the ocean floor. He and his team are looking for ways to mine it. In the course of my work I hope to gather solid evidence against unregulated mining. But we'll be doing that part of the research very quietly."

Karen studied him, looking for more.

"There's much that the average citizen, or even the avid student of oceanography, can't see at all. With literally billions if not trillions of dollars of riches to be gained, the biggest mining companies are being very successful and devious in blocking government regulation at all levels. But it is most certainly not over."

"I can just imagine," she muttered.

"I wish I could share with you certain new developments of great import, but you will have to wait. I can tell you one thing, though. For all the oceans there is bright new hope. Technology just might save the day after all." He paused. "So. Do you still have interest in going to sea with me this summer?"

She eyed him. "You have me hooked," she admitted, smiling at the pun.

And now here she was, on a clear June morning with her university spring classes finished – a hundred miles off-shore over the Pacific, her body strapped tightly in the back of a helicopter, seated next to Professor Blake as they flew to rendezvous with *Aladdin*. The ship was already underway, proceeding southwest to the Clarion-Clipperton Zone, a seabed covered with rich minerals.

The weather was beautiful, the sky cloudless. Karen's heart was pounding. She was just a lowly intern on this summer project, but her mentor sitting beside her was this famous deep-sea researcher. He had taken a strong liking to her which she at first had feared was sexual attraction, and she surely had no sexual interest in this middle-aged and somewhat pompous oceanography expert.

Flying over the Pacific at 5000 feet, the view from the window revealed an ocean of deep blue, highlighted by brilliant whitecaps. Karen felt her whole body being massaged by the steady vibration created by the rotors. And then the Professor started speaking to her through the helicopter headphones.

"You're going to meet some interesting people on this cruise," he was saying. "I've already told you a little bit about Aaron Kline. He's the Chief Scientist and an old friend of mine. He is a serious scholar and a good teacher. You'll learn a lot from him, and he's bringing along a number of nationally-known scientists plus several promising doctoral candidates, people you'll want to get to know."

"I'm so thankful for all of this," Karen responded.

"Oh, and the Captain of the ship is a fellow named Duke Pearson. I've known Duke for a long time too. He's a former Navy salvage expert who also did demolition work. Don't be put off by his gruff manner. He knows as much as anyone about deep-ocean seamanship.

"By the way, have you ever been at sea before?"

She tried to smile. "No – never."

Karen didn't connect the whitecaps to rough weather until the helicopter descended to several hundred feet over the water in preparation for its approach. The good ship *Aladdin*, a full 340 feet long, was pitching into the rough seas. Conditions were just within limits for landing. The pilot approached the pad and then put the helo into a nauseating climb away from the flight deck to circle for a second attempt. The pilot flew straight in, dropped and bounced down hard onto the deck. Karen was gripping her seat so tightly that her fingers went numb.

After the helicopter lifted off, *Aladdin* turned into the trough to proceed to the research site. The ship was now taking deep rolls as the two new arrivals were escorted down a narrow passageway. Karen found herself pitching into the bulkheads each step of the way, following a sailor who was having every bit as much ambulatory difficulty as she was.

They staggered into the ship's dining area, the crew's mess deck. Several men standing around the coffee urn reflexively stared at the new arrivals, focusing mainly on Karen, stripping her with their eyes. A short balding man sporting an unusually large gray mustache entered, looking for Blake.

"Ah, here you are," he said to Blake with the overtly arrogant amusement some mariners enjoy when confronted by passengers who have little experience at sea. Gripping the Professor's hand firmly, he smirked: "Gordon, how did you enjoy the flight out and the landing?"

"Good to see you, Duke." He turned to Karen. "This is Karen Finch, one of my more promising students and my intern on this cruise. Karen, this is the Captain, Duke Pearson."

Pearson's smile vanished. "You know, Gordon, your guest is the only female we have aboard. Just keep her out of the way." He stared at Karen. "I need to get to the bridge. You'll be escorted to your rooms. Talk later."

He turned on his heel and vanished through the forward door. Feeling definitely put off by the man, Karen watched him go. "Well this might become the longest three weeks of my life," she muttered.

"Please, don't let Duke get to you. He talks like a misogynist, even claims he left the Navy because there were, in his words, 'too many damn women.' Sadly, his devotion to his Navy career cost him his marriage. He's a complicated man, but it's all just talk. You'll do best to simply avoid him. He has his job to do and you have yours. Besides, on this cruise he works for me. Remember, Aaron and I have chartered this ship and the deep-dive equipment under contract for three months. This is entirely our show."

As the Professor was talking, Karen caught sight of another man entering the big dining room. He was looking for coffee, but observing the new arrivals, he turned to join them.

"Welcome aboard. I'm Charlie Hale, the communications officer, and you, I assume, are Professor Blake."

"That's correct. And I'd like to introduce you to Karen Finch, my summer intern."

"Welcome, Karen. You are in for quite an adventure. This is cutting edge work over perhaps the richest mineral field in the world. I am grateful to be a part of this effort, and I know you will be, too."

Karen couldn't resist asking, "What does the communications officer do?"

He smiled, appreciating the opportunity to share. "Because we are operating with tight controls over personal cell phone traffic, I am responsible for all the messages between ship and shore." He laughed. "Although the Captain and a select few have radio communications of their own, most of our messages are emails I deliver on paper to those who have permission to see them."

He fixated on Karen. He seemed different from the other men, not ogling her because she was a female in male territory, there was something more. It made her a little uncomfortable. However, his enthusiasm was catching.

The conversation was interrupted when the cook approached the Professor and Karen with an offer of coffee and a sandwich which both politely rejected. Karen was already feeling more than a bit unsettled in her stomach. Eating anything seemed impossible. A sailor appeared to escort them off down interior corridors to their staterooms. Because she was in fact the only woman on board and in spite of being a mere intern, she was among the privileged to occupy a double room all by herself.

After leaving the Professor at his door, she was all alone. She sat on her bunk, taking in the steady rumble of the engines, observing the strange empty surroundings of her small room, and bracing against the endless heaving and rolling. It was all slightly claustrophobic. Add the feeling of being a major inconvenience on board a ship full of overly eager men; it all started to depress her mood.

The decks had been declared off limits due to the high seas, so she was virtually a prisoner in her quarters. Her efforts to unpack were abandoned when the giant ship took a roll, and she fell hard against an open drawer. Then, as she was trying to read on her bunk, feeling more and more nauseated, there came a slight knock on the door. Before she could respond, the door opened slightly and someone called out:

"Karen, are you in here?"

There appeared a shock of blond hair and the bearded profile of a face she vaguely recognized. And then without further warning in walked that same cocky attractive doctoral candidate whose name she still didn't know. What? Him here? But at this low point she could not have been happier to see a fellow student. In spite of her nausea, her expression brightened.

He smiled back, noting how really beautiful she looked, her silky brown hair pulled back from her oval face revealing hazel eyes which were now intently studying him – eyes with a special gleam he hadn't noticed before.

"So," he went on, "I was just wondering if you finally have time to talk, or do you have to catch a bus?" He said this playfully. "Actually the Professor asked me to look in on you. He's deep into some meeting."

She spontaneously laughed. "Come on in. I'm so surprised to see you, but I'm also really glad to see a somewhat familiar face. I almost didn't recognize you with that beard. How long have you been on this ship?"

"I've been aboard about a month. Gordon Blake must think very highly of you to bring you along."

"He's working hard to turn me into a deep-water oceanographer, but so far, this voyage has convinced me that the ecology of small ponds would be much more to my liking."

"You'll get used to it, and you'll find the work fascinating. The weather's going to improve tomorrow. I'll give you the cook's tour, which reminds me, have you had dinner?"

"Oh! Ugh!" Karen was aware of the bile rising in her throat. She staggered to her feet and pushed by her visitor toward the crews' bathroom, the head, down the passageway. He watched her disappear, and then laughed to himself: "She has more excuses to run away than anyone I know!"

He decided not to embarrass her by waiting for her to return to her stateroom. And indeed, she suffered considerably in the crew's head. After rinsing her mouth and wiping her face, she realized she still didn't know that young man's name.

Meanwhile, Gordon had barely dumped his baggage in his stateroom when Doctor Aaron Kline accosted him. The two men had literally grown up together, attending the same university and finding they shared the same passion for oceanography as they pursued their master's and doctoral degrees. Over time, 'Doctors Blake and Kline' became known as a team of specialists whose complementary work opened up a number of new fields in their science. Of late, however, Gordon had devoted his energies to raising funds for deep-sea research. The summer project was the culmination of a lifetime of effort to enlist support for descents into the unknown reaches of the world's oceans. Meanwhile, Aaron had turned to commercial work consulting with potential mining companies.

"Gordon, it is so good to see you." He grabbed Gordon's right hand in both of his own. "I was in the middle of something in the lab, or I would have met you on the flight deck." He was a kindly looking man with a large head and receding hairline. Thick glasses in a heavy frame bridged his nose. "I can't say often enough how grateful I am to be a part of this project. This is thrilling! If we achieve the kind of successes I think are possible, we'll perish from all the publishing we will have to do!"

Both men chuckled and Gordon replied, "You have done well here, Aaron, in spite of some demoralizing setbacks."

"We have had more than our share. But we're making progress, and I'm counting on a successful test dive tomorrow."

Jason proceeded to Blake's stateroom to give him his progress report. He made every effort to be optimistic. "Acknowledging that we've had more than our share of setbacks recently, with a successful new test dive tomorrow we'll be solidly back on track."

Blake frowned. "Yeah, I got the update. Bunch of unusual mechanical failures, but that's to be expected with prototypes, right? And we've worked with this crew several times before. The equipment should still be basically sound."

Jason hesitated to answer. "Well, I'm keeping a careful eye out. This is a big ship with lots of people from several research teams on board. Lots of things can still go wrong."

The professor eyed him. "Jason, what are you saying?"

"I'm just saying we need to keep our eyes open."

- 3 -

Day Two

~~~~~~~~~~~~~~~

Well before breakfast the next morning, the crew standing watch on the bridge was rewarded with a radiant sunrise behind them. The red sunset the night before had augured well for the next day's weather, and the inky blue sky brightening to the east behind a few smudges of cloud confirmed their expectations. The barometer was rising. The seas had settled into four-foot undulations and the ship was pitching gently.

Karen woke up disoriented at first, not recognizing where she was and instantly frightened by feeling her whole world rocking and rolling. But a deeply appreciated miracle had occurred. Her nausea was mostly gone. Feeling ravenous, she pulled on shirt and pants and made her way to the mess deck, eagerly inhaling the smell of coffee, bacon, and fresh-baked bread. The Professor welcomed her to his table.

"'Morning, Karen. Sleep well? We're approaching the Clarion-Clipperton Zone so things are going to get busy on board. I have some update meetings to attend so I've arranged a tour of the ship for you. He'll be here any minute. But eat first. Food never tastes better than it does at sea."

She was just finishing a hearty solitary breakfast when she heard that same voice and turned to see that same blond-haired guy standing behind her. "So," he said, "are you ready for our maritime stroll? We ought to get going. Things are going to start jumping around here."

Minutes later they stepped out on deck where a light breeze teased at her hair and intense sunshine made her squint. As soon as they were clear of the door she turned to face him, blocking his way.

"Far enough. Don't you think that after two encounters I ought to know who you are?"

He readily agreed. "I certainly do." She was standing very close to him, and he was enjoying their moment of intimacy while playing with her.

But at that point, a freckle-faced beanpole of a man, standing on the deck above them hailed him. "There you are! Doctor Kline needs you in the lab as soon as possible."

He pouted at the interruption. He wanted a little more time with her before the day overtook them. "Okay. Can you give Karen here a tour of your yacht?"

"Absolutely."

"Karen, this is Buddy Lipscomb, deep submersible operator extraordinaire. Buddy, meet Karen Finch, a graduate student with Professor Blake. Show her around, and keep a close eye on her, as she has a habit of disappearing."

With a quick smile he was gone.

Right then the ship lookout shouted, "Whales off port bow!"

The whale belonged to a pod making its way north, breaking the surface of the water and basking in summer sun. Karen and Buddy Lipscomb watched the whales in awe. Buddy was as thrilled by the sight as Karen. "That's a good omen if you believe in such things," he said. "They are renowned for diving to great depths, just like we are doing with our new equipment."

The pod was moving off toward the horizon. "Come on, I have something you need to see."

They walked aft past several labeled doors: Electronics Closet, Computer Room, and Winch House to the stern, to the fantail. On the main deck Karen saw a large A-frame winch used to lift its two deep-dive payloads off the deck and down into the water. Under it was a small bright-yellow submarine, tubular shaped like a giant vitamin capsule, with stubby wings that made it look a bit like a fantasy flying machine in a kid's cartoon.

Next to the sub was a curious device that looked like a giant sled with long arms. Buddy explained that it was to be used to recover mineral deposits from the ocean floor. These deposits were the shape and size of potatoes, the result of absorbing metals from seawater over literally millions of years. The goal for Frontier Explorers was to demonstrate that this piece of equipment could collect these deposits without serious damage to the ecology thousands of feet below.

Buddy acknowledged the presence of the sled, but he focused on the submersible.

"I must admit, I'm thrilled to finally be able to pilot this remarkable piece of equipment." His face was filled with pride and awe. "Along with our unmanned deep-dive sled, this submersible has features only dreamed about before now. It's the main reason we contracted the designers at Ocean Ventures. We call her 'Yellow Bird' because she's entirely self-propelled with remarkable endurance, depth and speed. She holds four people, and a great array of sensors."

"Who are the lucky ones," Karen put in, "who get to take a journey to the bottom?"

"I'm the operator of the sub so of course I go down together with my back-up pilot. Others will take turns as passengers once we complete this test run. Maybe even you'll get to come down with me at some point."

"Oh no," she reacted. "Me in that, down thousands of feet – no way."

Buddy grinned. "Just wait. The urge will grab you and down you'll go. I assure you it's safe. You can stand here and watch. I need to get ready for the dive."

Karen noticed that the open deck had a large space dedicated to monitoring the undersea surveillance equipment. The main deck aft sloped gently toward the water. She looked again at the submersible and marveled at the nerve it would take to drop into the ocean inside that tube ... and go down and down and down ...

Abandoned by Buddy, Karen took the opportunity to examine the ship. *Aladdin* for its size was compact, given the need for the A-frame and its payloads, the flight deck, and the superstructure topped by the pilothouse on the bridge. On that 02 level aft were the staterooms for the Captain, the Navigator, Professor Blake, Doctor Kline as well as the Control Room and the deck provided for helicopter operations. On the main deck were the spaces Karen and Buddy had passed. Below were the quarters for the research team and the crew as well as the galley and mess deck.

As *Aladdin* approached the research site, the A-frame was still being rigged. The work should have been done earlier, but the weather had precluded it. The A-frame alone weighed several tons, and rigging the cables required to hoist and then deploy the sub was heavy work, which had to be done on the open, sloping deck. It was not safe to attempt in the dark, and the seas the day before had been washing over the fantail. The waves had abated to the point that *Aladdin* was pitching slowly over the long, gentle rollers. When it was time for the launch, the captain would adjust the course to produce a compromise between pitch and roll that would mitigate the ship's motion even further.

Buddy was already prepared for the dive. He would be accompanied by a new member of the team, an African American named Derek Prescott. Derek was the project's backup submersible operator, a job he had campaigned for even though his previous contribution to the research effort had been his skill as a lab technician.

With five hours of daylight left, Buddy and Derek lowered themselves into the sub, sealing the hatch behind them. Communication cables connected to the sub were disconnected, and the Yellow Bird was ready to enter the water. Work on the A-frame was complete. The winch operator slowly swung the submersible astern, well clear of the hull.

"Prepared to lower away," the winch operator informed the two people in the sub. And with their vocal concurrence, the Yellow Bird was lowered and settled into the Pacific. As Karen watched with fascination and also apprehension, two divers jumped into the water to release the retaining hook, and the submarine was freed. Underwater communications were established as the last traces of the yellow hull vanished from sight. Two men were now on their way to the deep.

Karen turned to Professor Blake who was standing at her side. Something wasn't quite making sense to her. "You told me that several weeks ago *Aladdin* was doing dives with the sub. So why this test dive?"

"Well," Gordon said, hesitating slightly, "there have recently been slight troubles on dives. Communications have cut out, electrical power has been very briefly interrupted, and reliable equipment has been acting up a bit. We even had a scare with a potential leak that would have caused a catastrophic failure of the sub's integrity."

"That sounds terrible," Karen put in. "I remember that same scenario in the news where allegedly a private sub imploded while diving down to the Titanic."

"Fortunately in our case Buddy noticed a slight nick in the hatch seal before we launched. But who knows how it got there. Other research teams have used the Bird for dives with no problems, but prototypes can have glitches. We're just being a hundred percent sure before resuming our deeper research dives."

Karen was lost in reflection, rubbing her right hand over her left forearm, a habit she had developed as a child. "How do you know what has gone wrong if the operators can't communicate with you?"

"We have back up capabilities. For one thing, we track them with transponders, sound-emitting devices on the submarine's hull. *Aladdin* has a string of hydrophones, suspended at intervals down a long cable, which pick up the signals. Works most of the time if the temperature gradients in the water cooperate. The submersible is also equipped with buoys that the operator can release on a cable to the surface so that we can talk to them. As a safety feature they also have both pre-recorded messages and the capability to deliver recordings of the passengers' voices. If they can't reach us by underwater telephone for whatever reason, they can pop a buoy. Come on, let's head to the monitoring room."

The Control Room was a large dark space full of various electronics consoles, recording devices and an array of communications equipment. It took a moment to adjust to the blue, fluorescent light after the glare on deck. A dozen people were at work.

The submarine had been designed and built by a company called Ocean Ventures. Their representative, Simson Turner, spoke up to give the Professor a preliminary report.

"We have them on the UT." He turned to Karen. "Underwater transponder. They're just now descending through one thousand feet."

"Any problems?"

"No and I'm not expecting any."

Karen was captivated by a hologram presentation of the submarine in a large three-dimensional tube. Yellow Bird was depicted in a column of water. As the operator expanded the scale to show the entire depth from sea floor to sea surface, the sub became a grain of sand settling very slowly down into a very deep well.

A tinny voice cut in. *"Control, this is Buddy. We are approaching two thousand feet. Over."*

"This is Control. Roger. Hold at three thousand."

The operator adjusted the hologram scale again and the sub was seen sinking in a wide spiral. To Karen the spiraling hologram was mesmerizing.

"What are they seeing down there?" Karen queried.

"For the first few hundred feet," the Professor explained, "there is rapidly increasing darkness. They might see some marine life, but they'll have a better chance of seeing living things in the sub spotlights as they descend deeper."

"It must be so spooky down there."

"Once you get in deep water," Blake said, "because of all the bioluminescence, the sensation is like falling through the stars. Or so I'm told. I haven't been down myself."

They watched until they heard Buddy's voice again. *"Control, we are approaching three thousand feet. I'm now leveling the boat, engaging the propulsion drive, and preparing to deploy the handling equipment and hull cameras."*

Over half a mile below the ship, Buddy swept the arm to the right in awkward slow motion before reversing it. The claw disappeared from the camera view, then reappeared on its way to the left of the monitor.

"This is Buddy. The port camera is processing properly, but we do not have train and elevation; and the camera won't sync with the arm."

"Shift to the starboard camera and take a look at the handling equipment."

During the silence, Dr. Aaron Kline observed to no one in particular, "Damn. In the middle of our last dive the cameras wouldn't train and elevate, nor would they process moving objects. We thought it was a problem in the sub, but later we found that the computer up here was slightly mis-programmed. And once the sub is in the water, we can't change the computer settings."

"Control, the starboard camera tracks just fine."

"Good, so we only have one video problem to solve tonight."

As the room went quiet again. Karen asked: "Dr. Kline, how many people are working for you on this ship?"

"Please, call me Aaron. Most don't work for me." He smiled. "The captain and three officers oversee a crew of twenty-three sailors who stand bridge and engineering watches, serve in the galley and attend to the laundry among other things. There are six men on the equipment tech team, all hired by Frontier Explorers specifically to handle deep-ocean equipment. I and Gordon have embarked a dozen scientists and research technicians who ..."

"Control, this is Buddy. We cannot stow the port camera. All other checks are satisfactory. We are proceeding to dump ballast to return to the ship. Over."

After a short visit to the galley and a probe into the main research lab, Karen returned to the monitoring room to find out when they would be expecting Yellow Bird to surface. The complacency she had expected to find there had been supplanted by looks of alarm on the faces of the men surrounding the speaker to the underwater telephone. Before she could ask Aaron what had happened, Captain Pearson brushed past her. He wasted no time taking over.

"Quick – what depth are they at?"

"Buddy reported leaving three thousand feet," Aaron told him. "That squared with our display before we lost communications and the hologram."

"What exactly did he say before we lost them?"

Aaron turned to the voice-activated recorder. "Let me play it back for you. Notice the tone of voice."

Buddy's voice at first was calm: *"The starboard camera is picking up odd ripples of luminescence. It looks like a curtain. I'm going to turn on our lights to get a better look ..."*

The recording went silent for about thirty seconds before Buddy spoke again. *"The lights don't help – I can't tell what I'm seeing. It looks like a giant animal; it stretches into the murk to starboard and out of range of the lights. Derek sees the same thing out his window. I've never seen anything like it. I'm dropping more ballast. Wait – this thing is coming closer, moving faster now across our lights. I think I see a – what? It's suddenly – gone. No more luminescence at all."*

Buddy now shouted in a totally panicked voice at Derek: *"Speak up, do you see anything? Is there anything out there? What was –"*

There followed several minutes of indistinct mumbling – then sudden silence. The Captain seemed temporarily mute. Aaron abruptly shouted to the room, "Get Blake here – now. And if Buddy calls, respond evenly. Keep it cool. Business as usual."

He turned to Duke. "You know – we all know – we can't raise the sub."

Just then Buddy's voice interrupted further discussion: "*Control, this is Buddy. Do you hear me?*"

"This is Control. Are you two alright?"

Karen noticed that the hologram was again active.

"*Control, we are fine. I think we may have climbed above whatever it was we saw. We can't see anything through the ports or with the cameras.*"

"This is Control. Continue your ascent. The seas are abating and –"

"*Oh no – something is now lifting us!*"

The hologram showed the submersible pitching over, and then the image disappeared.

Aaron now grabbed the microphone, "Buddy, Derek, can you hear us?"

The seconds were audible on the ship's clock. Aaron handed the mike back to the telephone operator.

"Look!" someone shouted. "The hologram – the sub is upright and proceeding toward the surface!"

The underwater telephone cut in again: "*... this is Buddy. Do you hear me? We are back to level. Derek is bleeding badly from his forehead. I have the Bird in a* *climb. No ballast. Full power. Passing one thousand feet. I will check in again before breaching. Over."*

Aaron grabbed the microphone again. "Buddy, Derek, this is Aaron. I will have the doctor standing by for your return. Any leaks? Over."

"Aaron, this is Derek. We are 'ops normal.' She's a tough old Bird. No leaks as far as we can tell – and I think we would know."

The sub continued its steep ascent. Buddy cut the engine, leveled the submersible, and let Yellow Bird boil up the last two hundred feet to daylight.

Karen had been careful to remain well clear of the events taking place in the monitoring room, and when it appeared that the crisis was over, she proceeded to the deck to watch the recovery operation. The divers were getting suited up and the A-frame was positioned over the water. Fortunately the weather had abated to where the long swells would produce a minimum of turbulence for connecting the hoist to the sub.

Yellow Bird had no ballast and was rising twice her usual speed out of the deep at a steep angle. *"Control, this is Buddy. I am at two hundred feet and ... we're surfacing!"*

A crewman on the Signal Bridge atop the pilot house saw the upwelling about a hundred yards to the north. He shouted to get attention, and Karen saw the sub burst to the surface, heaving itself high in the water before settling as if to submerge, sending a huge ripple in all directions. *Aladdin* was immediately rumbling to close the distance, white water washing out from under her transom as the big screw bit into the ocean.

The approach to the submarine was professional, and the divers entered the water within a few yards of their quarry. In the relatively calm water they had little difficulty clipping the wire halyard onto the ring bolt mounted high on the sub hull. On signal, the winch operator tensioned the line, and the submersible rose up and cleared the water, to be lowered inches at a time to her cradle on deck.

Normally at this point Buddy would pop the hatch and emerge looking a bit like a beaming astronaut back from the moon. However, this time the hatch did not immediately open; and when it did, Derek instead of Buddy appeared, with drying blood covering most of the left half of his face.

"Buddy's in too much pain to climb the ladder. You're going to have to lift him out."

In sick bay it was found that Derek had only a superficial head wound. Buddy, on the other hand, had two bruised ribs and a sprained wrist. After supervising the evacuation of the sub, Captain Pearson turned to Simson Turner, "You designed the sub. I want you to go over that boat with a magnifying glass. I want to know if anything – anything – isn't right with it. We are supposed to dive again tomorrow and that's what I plan to do."

The Captain went down to sick bay to see how his operators were doing. Meanwhile Aaron and

Gordon were having a hushed one-on-one discussion about what had happened, and how this would impact the next day's dive. The temporary loss of their best operator and the uncertainty about the condition of the Bird weighed heavily on them.

Ten minutes later the two leaders of the project decided to sideline the sub for tomorrow. It was not a setback. They were eager to deploy the instrument sled that some wag had nicknamed Trilobite because it had tentacle-like arms and long grasping claws that recalled the pre-historic ocean dweller.

The sled was capable of the same depths as its sophisticated cousin, and had the added advantage of being connected by cable to monitors on board *Aladdin*. This meant that the control team could manipulate the sled to targets of their choosing. And of equal importance, the sled was unmanned, so greater risks could be taken with it when approaching the bottom. With the decision made, the two research heads told the watch officer to have the tech team prepare Trilobite for a dive.

Aaron and Gordon then headed off to talk with the submersible operators. Derek was sleeping, they didn't disturb him. Buddy, however, was wide awake, sitting up against a bank of pillows and reading. He spoke with a whisper, careful not to exercise his ribcage any more than he had to.

"Good to see you're doing okay," Aaron said to him. "I know you're in pain. Right now all we need to know is if you think there is a problem with the Bird."

Buddy suddenly looked desperate. He clearly had something to say. After a moment he whispered: "There is nothing … wrong with the Bird … but you must find out what's … down there!"

"We will, Buddy. We will. We're sending down the sled tomorrow. You just concentrate on getting better."

"Captain, I've checked out the submersible from top to bottom," Simson informed Duke in his cabin. "The hull is intact, and from what I can tell on deck, all systems are functioning except for the port camera. But there is one thing that disturbs me."

Simson hesitated.

"Go on – what is it?" Duke pushed him.

"Well when we looked into the ballast bay we found that the hooks that release the ballast weights … well, over half of them were bent out of line. Buddy shouldn't have been able to release the ballast, and if he hadn't been able to, the sub probably wouldn't have made it back to the surface."

"That doesn't make sense. Get the hooks fixed, but before you do, photograph the entire sub inside and out, just in case there's a claim by Ocean Ventures later on. Oh, and don't tell the research team about the ballast problem. They're already squeamish about using the sub."

Simson nodded as he left but stopped at the cabin door. "I almost forgot to tell you. We found some gelatinous stuff sticking to the starboard propeller mount. We're cleaning it off. It stinks! Smells like rotten eggs."

- 4 -

The Encounter

~~~~~~~~~~~~~~~~

By sunrise the handling crew and lab technicians had completed preparations for deploying the sled. Karen had risen early and gone off to observe the preparations. The Professor had suggested that, as his intern, she should learn all she could about every aspect of the research. She was welcomed there by the handling team leader, Jonas Pennypacker. As they were finishing the last of their checklists and rigging chores, she was handed a hot cup of coffee to celebrate the Early-Bird reward of a spectacular sky brightening rapidly with color.

Heading down to join the watch team in the monitoring room, Karen found Aaron briefing the team: "... so, given the decision to send the sled to the bottom, we want to confirm that we are, in fact, over a rich harvest of minerals. Today's dive will commence at 7:30. So, good luck." And under his breath he muttered, "to all of us."

Karen had been so occupied with the events taking place aboard *Aladdin* that she'd forgotten to rendezvous with her blond-haired tour guide whose name she still didn't know. As she hurried to the mess hall she almost ran right into him in a hallway.

"Oh!" she said. "There you are."

He looked flustered. "Sorry, but I've got to cancel again," he told her rapidly. "I'm now slotted to be a passenger, supercargo as they call it, for the next Bird descent. I need to spend most of today with Aaron and in Yellow Bird preparing for the assignment."

"I understand."

"I rather doubt if you do, things are so complex right now," he retorted. "Look, I do want to find time to spend with you, but today and probably all of tomorrow are out. I'm sure the Professor will keep you busy with something. Gotta run now."

And with that, he was gone. She stood there alone in the hallway, a bit stunned by his news. And as she imagined him climbing down into the Bird tomorrow morning, she realized for the first time that she was actually becoming somewhat emotionally attached to that young man.

The first progress report on the sled was scheduled for 10:00 am sharp. The sled had been deployed for over two hours. "Aaron, we have crossed and re-crossed this patch of the bottom, and there is no sign of the minerals we expected to see in abundance."

The Chief Scientist frowned. "How can that be?"

The man in charge of the team on watch responded. "This leads me to wonder if the map is accurate, or if perhaps there's a navigational problem here or on the sled. When we retrieve the sled tonight we'll find out what went wrong. Tomorrow we'll need to send the sled down again to validate the location. If it's accurate, we'll send the Bird."

Following a very brief conversation with the Professor about her unfolding role as intern on the ship, Karen spent her morning in the lab in an effort to learn more about the discoveries the research team had made to date. There she had the opportunity to meet three more PhD candidates, Carl Ambrose, Billy McCullough, and Julian Phelps, each of whom in turn served as watch supervisors for the research team. They went out of their way to make her feel welcome.

The lab technicians were also generous with their extensive explanations. So far this voyage had yielded a variety of marine life, including tube worms, white crabs and sea anemones that dwell in deep waters adjacent to hot vents.

"As the Earth's magma wells out of the ocean floor," one of the men was telling her, "it heats the water to temperatures well above the surface boiling point of 212 degrees Fahrenheit. The chemicals in the water precipitate similar to how they do with geyser formations on land. Over time these chemicals produce solid towers up to several stories high – thus creating a unique environment for the special flora and fauna their ecology supports in the black water over a mile below the ocean's surface."

And on and on the lecture went, most of which Karen already knew from related graduate courses she'd taken. After two hours and all the biology and chemistry lessons Karen could absorb, she excused herself to proceed aft where she hoped to get a look at the interior of Yellow Bird.

She wasn't disappointed, for she found Derek overseeing equipment checks. He was a handsome man in his early thirties with a receding hairline that made him look quite mature. He was almost six feet tall, and stocky. She wondered how he could fit into the submersible that was cradled in front of them.

"That's good," he was saying on an intercom to someone inside the Bird. "Now press the stick to starboard."

"Done."

He was watching his laptop screen. "Okay. That should wrap it up." He turned to Karen. "Oh, hi. You must be Professor Blake's intern." He reached to shake her hand. "I'm Derek Prescott."

"I'm Karen Finch – so good to meet you, especially after yesterday."

His expression became slightly quizzical. "That sounds ominous, like you're surprised I'm still here." He capped that comment with a bright smile.

"No. No. That's not what I meant. But based on the amount of blood I saw on your face when you surfaced, I didn't expect you'd be back at work so soon. You and Buddy were very brave."

"Whoa!" He laughed, "A hero I'm not. Frankly, we were scared shitless, pardon my French. Whatever that was down there, I'm hoping it was a once-in-a-lifetime encounter. I'd never seen anything like it – anywhere."

"So, you'll go again?"

"Of course." He patted the sub. "I have every confidence in the Bird. And even if I didn't want to go, I don't think I'd have a choice. Buddy is down for the count. Captain Pearson and Doctor Kline are going to have to use their second-string quarterback, stitches and all." He impishly fingered the bandage over his left eye.

Unseen by Karen, the operator down in the sub emerged from the hatch. He was about to say something to Derek when he noticed the woman – and stepped back down a rung to observe her surreptitiously rather than interrupt them. She seemed to be in a cheerful mood but her dark eyebrows made her look serious.

As he dropped down out of sight, the sound of the radio on his belt made him jump.

"Hey down there," Derek was saying, "are you ready for a visitor?"

"Sure. Send ... him down."

"Not him, her. Karen Finch, the Prof's intern. She's on her way." He turned to Karen. "The first part of this little tour is the most critical." He pointed. "That hatch holds out literally tons of water pressure when we're working the ocean floor. Don't touch the seal and don't ding the hatch as you pass through. I'm glad to see you aren't wearing a watch. If you don't mind, I'll take your belt until you're back on deck."

Karen complied and then climbed up the ladder to the submarine's small entry deck. The hatch tower stuck up another eighteen inches, providing space for the hatch mechanism and seals. Derek called up to her from the deck. "This is the tricky part. Turn so that you can place one foot over the combing onto the top rung. Grab the tower rim. Good. Now lift your other leg over. Okay. And now back down the ladder."

Karen did as she was told, descending out of the sun's glare into the sub's dim interior, looking down and watching her feet descend into the shadows. When she reached the bottom of the short ladder she felt strong fingers grab her right arm, steadying her.

"Watch your head!" the man said. She turned and saw him there, smiling warmly. "Welcome to my alterworld."

"Oh! It's you!"

"Is that bad?"

"No, no, of course not. I didn't mean it that way."

They were standing quite close; it was an intimate breathless moment. "Hold on," she said, "Not another word until you tell me your name. This has gone on long enough. It's silly." She laughed. "I'm afraid we'll get interrupted again."

He grinned impishly. "I'm Jason Crocker."

She extended her hand to shake. "Pleased to meet you, Jason Crocker. So, are you actually thinking of going down in this thing – thousands – of feet – tomorrow?"

"Yes. If it's ready to go, I'll join Derek for the dive. It'll be my first time, an opportunity of a lifetime. This sub is awesome. Let me show you."

"Please do."

He put his hand on her arm and pulled her gently to a position next to him in the tight space. "This is the diving-controls indicator panel."

He pointed out the instruments he was familiar with and answered her questions as best he could. He admitted that much of the interior was unfamiliar to him. His candor didn't quench her curiosity. She was quick, intuitive, and focused – and he felt captivated by her business-like approach to discovering the secrets of the submersible.

While he was enjoying his quite natural manly but professionally discouraged feelings provoked by her tantalizing presence in such close quarters, she was hiding her own similar feelings by concentrating on learning as much as she could about the Bird as quickly as possible. She doubted that she would get another chance to see the interior again, much less ever make the dive the Professor had promised.

And to be honest, she was studying Jason closely as he spoke. He seemed quite modest, intelligent, and also amusing. He had a lightness to his mood, a sense of being comfortable inside his own skin, that she was strongly attracted to. His eyes were gentle, not overtly probing – but she suspected he missed very little. Then, for just a fleeting flash she found herself wondering what it would be like to kiss a man with a beard.

When they got to the front of the small cabin, Jason urged her to sit where the pilot of a dive manipulated the controls. She took the seat eagerly and upon his direction, gripped the control stick. He kneeled in the narrow isle, put his right hand on the back of the seat and placed his left hand over hers, noting that her hand felt smooth and cool. It was the first time they'd touched – and they both were touched.

Karen glanced at him and she had to smile. "You really are an operator, aren't you."

"Oh, not really," he smiled back at her.

Karen broke the spell and asked: "So tell me, I heard that there had been some communication and electrical problems. Professor Blake told me about the seal. Is all this stuff normal?"

He made no effort to delude her. "No, Karen, it's not. We have had an exceptional run of bad luck." He shrugged. "Nothing we can't overcome. I'm really proud of the way that Gordon and Aaron have kept this project going." He offered nothing further.

Meanwhile over two miles beneath them the sled continued its laborious sweep through the ocean, a hundred feet above the seafloor. At noon Aaron checked with the watch to see if they had made any progress – then went to lunch. Blake and Kline had agreed earlier that if there was no progress with the search by one o'clock they would focus attention for the rest of the day investigating more fully yesterday's accident, as it was officially being labeled. They knew that Frontier Explorers would want a detailed accounting. The injuries to the submersible operators might incur insurance claims. And the question of programmer error, or worse, also lingered in the air.

Beyond the practical requirements of detailing the events, the scientists and indeed everyone on the ship wanted to know what it was that Buddy and Derek had seen down below. In order to assure themselves that the right technical questions were posed, and to avoid second-guessing by Frontier Explorers, they invited the Captain and also Simson Turner to join them.

Derek was called in first. A video camera recorded the interview, and Jason was asked to take additional notes. After identifying himself to the camera, Derek was asked to give his description of the dive, starting with the launch. Because Buddy had been the operator, his memory of the descent was largely an account of what he saw outside the small port in the hull.

However, when they asked him about the equipment checks he said: "The port camera was a problem. It never worked right. I had personally operated both cameras early that morning using the computer in the monitoring room. I also filmed the handling crew at work on the sub, and everything was fine."

"Were there any indications that there would be problems as you descended?"

"No, and we haven't found anything wrong mechanically with the equipment. It's all part of a giant computer network, so we could be dealing with a software glitch. That said, Frontier Explorers has been using this network for several years without mishap.

"So tell us," the Captain insisted, "was there anything unusual about your upward departure from 3000 feet?"

"Well as you and the others know, Buddy was being very careful to ascend without doing further damage to the port camera."

Simson asked: "How fast were you ascending?"

"Buddy was dumping ballast, but we were still climbing all too slowly. I didn't want to second-guess him, but it was going to take a lot more than ninety minutes to breach, and then when we saw whatever that thing was, I forgot all about our ascent speed."

Gordon jumped in. "So exactly what did you see?"

"Professor, it's what I didn't see." Derek's eyes fixed on him. "Buddy started to get really excited about something he'd picked up on the starboard camera. He turned on the searchlights, and reported to you that he and I were both watching something out our ports. But I can't tell you now whether I was seeing something living or just weird murk. There was bioluminescence but that's normal. What wasn't normal was that at some point the surrounding water got suddenly entirely dark, like someone had turned out the lights."

"What did you think at the time?"

"I don't remember thinking anything. Buddy became very excited at that point. He kept asking me what I saw – and I kept telling him, 'Nothing.'"

"There was an interval there where we couldn't raise you. Several minutes went by. What was going on?"

"We kept trying to raise Control. Buddy settled down. The blackness didn't appear to be threatening. Everything else seemed normal, so we figured we'd just keep heading for the surface."

"Weren't you worried about not being able to talk to us?"

"It happens. Water is a tough medium to work through. Sound does funny things. We've experienced times on earlier dives when we couldn't communicate with Control even though we were less than a thousand yards from the ship's hydrophone array."

Aaron then asked: "Buddy reported that you had climbed above whatever it was he'd seen, and that he didn't see anything out of the ports. Did he mean he didn't see any marine life – or that you were still in blackness?"

Derek took a moment to remember. "The ocean was as dark as I've ever seen it."

"What happened next?"

"Just after we regained contact with you, all of a sudden, as if we were being lifted by an overtaking wave, the sub pitched downward while the stern kept rising. We somersaulted – but I don't know why."

The Captain had been listening to the proceedings intently. He leaned forward on his elbows and stared at Derek. "You have already told us that Buddy was rattled. You also said that he was being really cautious about the ascent. Could he have pushed the diving planes and accelerated the submersible in such a fashion as to create the accident?"

"Buddy? Never – he's a pro! But that's not the point, Captain. The Bird went through a 360-degree somersault, it was way too tight for an operator to create. It would be physically impossible."

"Well damnit, what other alternative is there?"

Derek hesitated. After all the earlier questions, they had finally gotten down to it. He said flatly: "I can only surmise that we were attacked."

The room fell silent. Every man there had considered that same possibility with varying degrees of disbelief. Now that Derek had said it out loud, they were going to have to discuss it.

Simson was the first to speak. "Derek, I've been in this business a long time. We encountered a lot of strange things, as Duke here can confirm, but nothing we ever encountered posed a risk to our submersibles. Surface ships have been rammed by whales, and submarines have had close calls with ice. Are you suggesting that something physical came up behind you and pitchpoled the boat? Why would anything do that?"

Before Derek could collect his thoughts to answer, Aaron cocked his head at Duke. "I think it's unfair to ask him why, but it's definitely germane to this investigation to ask how."

He looked back at Derek. "Please, describe in greater detail what you and Buddy experienced during the incident?"

"Like I said, the sub's stern started to rise and the bow pitched down. It felt like we were being pushed through the water as we nosed down. Once we passed vertical, Buddy and I both fell onto the control console and rolled onto the overhead and the sub kept rolling over. We fell off the overhead into the rear of the cabin. That's where I hit my head and Buddy banged his ribs and I landed on his wrist. Then as fast as it had begun, the sub suddenly righted itself."

The Captain frowned, then he grudgingly accepted Derek's account. "Well, given the fact that you got the submersible back intact, you did the right thing."

Gordon added, "I think all of us appreciate what an awful experience you had yesterday, but it still leaves open the question regarding what you encountered. I assume that you saw a large marine creature. What I want to know is, has anyone ever seen the likes of it before?"

Derek smiled the first smile of the afternoon. "And my question is, will we ever have to encounter another one again?"

The investigation digressed into a roundtable discussion about the myths and realities of large marine life. Although not everyone fully subscribed to the theory that the submersible had been attacked, there was general consensus that it had been rolled by some living thing. Whales were suggested, as were giant squid, because they were among the few large ocean dwellers that the experts knew could reach the deep ocean.

But no one considered that perhaps they were examining this problem from the wrong perspective. The creature might have in fact risen from the depths.

Derek's interview was just finished when word arrived from McCullough, the watch supervisor, that the sled had located a mineral field. "All the signs are good – patches of clear water, a concentration of marine life, and the nodules scattered everywhere."

"Alright!" Aaron said. "We're on for tomorrow."

- 5 -

The Hearing

~~~~~~~~~~~~~~~~

Karen started her day just as she had the day before. She rose before dawn and washed her face at a sink in the crew's head. As she walked out to observe preparations to send down the sled to the new location, she could feel the ship gently wallowing in an almost flat ocean.

On deck before even a hint of dawn, she was stunned by the spectacle that greeted her as she stepped through the door onto the main deck. Nothing she had ever seen before prepared her for the sheer number of stars twinkling brightly through the clear ocean air above her. She stepped to the rail and lifted her face in silent wonder, enthralled by thousands of constellations and the spread-out celestial cloud of the Milky Way overhead.

Any sense of urgency she had felt to go aft and watch the men preparing the sled disappeared. Instead she stood gazing upward for a long time, keenly aware that she was experiencing the point of separation between two vastly different worlds – sky and sea. So little was known about either one. And how ironic, she thought to herself, all alone on deck, that both deep space and deep ocean visually sparkled in the absence of the sun.

Then suddenly her peaceful solitary reverie was broken by the tiny arc and sizzle of a glowing cigarette butt that had been flicked off the bridge wing into the water in front of her. She turned fast and looked up at the dark silhouette of a man – who immediately pivoted to reenter the pilothouse. For no reason she found herself shivering, feeling exposed – watched. And for just a moment she found herself actually afraid on this big unfamiliar ship – then she pushed away her gut reaction.

After watching the sled get prepped by half a dozen alert guys moving through their tight-tech pre-launch procedures, she proceeded to breakfast. She was greeted heartily by Professor Blake. She responded with a desultory "hi."

"Why, Karen," Gordon reacted, "I thought you were a morning person. You're not getting seasick again, are you?"

She smiled thinly. "No. I had a great time working with the handling crew yesterday, but I don't think I need to make that a daily ritual. The technical checks are boring. I should be spending more time in the lab and the monitoring room. After all, you brought me here to learn about deep water oceanography, not deck seamanship."

They were joined by Jason, who greeted Karen with an apology for missing dinner with her the night before. "I spent the afternoon preparing experiments for my dive and just lost track of the time," he told her. "It was almost eight o'clock when I finished."

Feeling more cheerful in his presence, Karen laughed lightly and shook her head. "No problem, there were plenty of guys to chat with over dinner."

Gordon spoke up: "Jason, you are everything a scholar should be – you're the consummate PhD. Hey, that rhymes." He smiled expansively.

"You're in an awfully good mood today," Jason responded, a bit bashful about being praised.

"After yesterday's debacle, we can only do better. If all goes well today, then down you go tomorrow to explore what the sled discovered. You feeling ready?"

"Nothing would please me more. So is Buddy going to be able to make the dive?"

"I just checked. He'll be nursing those ribs for at least a week, but we have his stand-in. Which reminds me, we're going to interview Buddy after breakfast. Since you'll be making the next dive, I'd like to have you hear what he has to say."

Karen asked, "How did it go with Derek?"

"He didn't seem rattled by the test dive," Gordon told her. "He'll be fine tomorrow."

"But, what about the giant ... well, that giant whatever they saw?"

"He was vague about that, although he thinks the sub was being *attacked*. We'll ask Buddy. But please," he urged her, "Derek's 'attack' comment must remain *strictly* between us. Okay?"

"Well, of course. But what kind of giant creature could live at those depths? What would possibly attack a submersible the size of the Bird? Has this kind of thing happened before?"

"Please, enough on that topic."

The conversation went off into other pressing dive themes, but Karen's mind wouldn't let go of the idea of a monster down below her, perhaps right now. Then she tuned back into what Jason and Gordon were discussing.

"... and then we'll just see what kind of a sea bottom we're dealing with. We also want to create a temperature profile and see if we can learn more about the mantle." Gordon anticipated the reaction he saw in Jason's eyes. "I know it's more geology than oceanography. But we're not done. You may find those mineral samples yield new opportunities for your microbiology research."

A young man approached the trio and spoke to the Professor. "Excuse me, sir. They're ready to launch the sled, moving through the pre-flight brief just now."

Gordon excused himself, reminding Jason to be back in the dining area at 8:30 for the Lipscomb debriefing. Karen was invited to observe.

On order from the Captain, the crew's mess was cleared of people lingering over coffee, and the entry door closed to discourage interruptions. Right on time, basically the same group who had interviewed Derek the day before filed into the mess hall and sat down around the captain's table to query Buddy – Professor Blake, Captain Pearson and Simson Turner. Jason and Karen were present.

Gordon formally officiated as he had the day before, starting the recorder and turning to Buddy. "So, we interviewed Derek yesterday to hear what he had to say about the dive that took place on June twenty-ninth. Now we need to hear from you. You are asked to describe the sub's performance as you two descended."

"Yes, sir. I've done a number of dives with the submersible and the dive on the twenty-ninth started off no different than any other. We were 'ops normal' to three thousand feet."

"What was the first indication that not everything was working properly?"

"As I reported to you, the port camera wouldn't follow the claw arm."

Simson spoke up. "Do you have any theories why that was happening?"

Buddy did not answer right away. His brush with the large fish had pushed these more mundane issues out of his mind. "I haven't given the port camera much thought in the past two days, but there are really two things to consider. Either the camera itself was damaged or in some way incapable of movement, or the commands loaded into the program were flawed. You'd have to do a process of elimination."

"We have inspected the mechanical arm. It's fine – and the software checks so far have revealed nothing out of the ordinary. Is it possible that you were distracted and failed to operate the controls properly?"

It was a bald question. Couched differently, Buddy might have been willing to consider it; but Simson's use of the words 'failed' and 'distracted' were deeply insulting. He answered earnestly, his voice tight. "Simson, I've worked on submersibles a long time, not as long as you for sure, but certainly long enough to know how to operate the equipment. I can do camera work in my sleep. Why would you think I could be distracted when I was in the middle of a sea trial and the camera was the object of my attention?"

Simson was not convinced. "Sorry, but it's the only option that makes sense."

Gordon didn't like the bickering. "Let's move on. I don't want to get bogged down." He looked over the top of his reading glasses. "Buddy, you've probably heard that the sled is currently on its way to the bottom, and I'm hoping against hope that we find the mineral field we located yesterday. Right now I want to concentrate on what it is you saw on the way back to the surface."

Captain Pearson and Simson were both surprised by the Professor's shift. They urgently wanted to find out if Buddy had thought there was anything wrong with the Bird's performance, and whether he would mention a problem with the ballast.

But Gordon persevered. "I want you to listen to the audio as you and Derek ascended."

Everyone listened in rapt attention as Buddy's tech-scratchy voice came alive on the speakers: *"... I can't tell what I'm seeing. It looks like it's all part of a single animal. It stretches into the murk to starboard and out of range of the lights. Derek sees the same thing out his window."*

Gordon turned off the recording. Everyone sat in silence for a moment. Then he asked, "Buddy, can you tell us anything more than you did then?"

The question animated the experienced sub pilot. "Well whatever it was, it was huge. I haven't thought about much else since we got back. I keep thinking that we were looking at a living wall. I still can't figure out why the lights didn't show us more. It sounds bizarre but my best guess is that the thing was bigger than the spread of the illumination."

"Go on."

"Well – then it very quickly disappeared into the murk on my side of the sub. Did you ask Derek what he thought about its size?"

"In his debriefing," Gordon said evenly, "Derek said he isn't sure he saw anything."

"But he *told* me he saw something. I grabbed his arm to get his attention, pointed at my window and asked him if his window looked the same – and he nodded."

"Okay. Let's play the next piece."

"I've never seen anything like it. I'm dropping more ballast – this thing is close! It's moving faster now,

across our lights. I think I see a – oh, now it's disappearing."

Gordon stopped the recording. "What did you think you saw?"

Buddy stared right through him. "The curtain of lights I saw, it started moving. The bright pinpoints started to blur a bit. It appeared to be tapering down with fewer lights top and bottom, maybe I was seeing a tail. I thought I maybe saw a fin."

"Can you be more specific?"

"Specific? I don't know … it could have been a gigantic fin along the top of the tail. And then it was just – gone."

"And a short time later you came back on the audio and started shouting. Here's that recording:

"Something is lifting us – we're pitching over – I can't hold on …"

Gordon stopped the recording again. He was staring at Buddy. "So, what do you think was happening?"

"Well if Derek and I had been sitting in a car, it would have been the same feeling if someone had picked up the rear fenders and flipped the car over lengthwise onto its roof. And then the sub continued to roll over until we were upright again. I can't imagine the size of a creature that could do that."

"So tell me now, do you think something down there actually attacked the sub?"

Buddy paused to consider his answer. "I know it seems pretty silly, but there only seems to be two possibilities – either we were purposely attacked, or something ridiculously big accidentally bumped into the sub. All I know for certain is that there was something very large in the water with us down there."

He fell silent. "Is that all?" the Professor asked him.

"Yes. I think so."

"Thank you. Does anyone else have any questions they want to ask about this encounter?"

There was a noise behind them. Gordon turned his head toward the door. A seaman had burst into the room.

"Sir, you are requested by the watch supervisor."

The Captain jumped in. "I have one question before we go." He turned to Buddy. "Was there anything in the submersible's performance that would lead you to question your last conclusion? In other words, is it possible that through a combination of commands to the sub you could have induced the somersault? Have you in your experience with the boat harbored any doubts about its stability?"

Buddy swallowed. "I am extremely careful to operate the Bird so as to never generate extreme stress and perhaps threaten you or Frontier Explorers. And within those always-cautious parameters I have no doubts regarding its stability. There's something else going on, and right now I have no idea what that is. We can proceed, in my opinion, but cautiously."

The Captain nodded at Buddy and looked to the Professor, who lost no further time concluding the interview. Everyone followed him out, leaving the mess suddenly abandoned except for the scullery crew banging pots and pans in the galley.

- 6 -
The Tower

~~~~~~~~~~~~~~~~

The atmosphere in Control was permeated with excitement. The sled had been searching for ninety minutes when the first indications of a hot vent were apparent to the Control operators aboard *Aladdin*. McCullough got the Professor and the Captain up to speed while Jason and Karen listened.

"In the process of scanning the bottom, we've located a vent. A closer look at the sea floor around it shows abundant life including ten-foot tube worms, giant clams, purple octopuses, and pale anemones."

As they watched, bright red shrimp swam across the screen, as if on cue. "Well done, Billy. Have you found a chimney?"

"I'm guessing the vent should be about thirty yards dead ahead."

The sled's slow movement was being recorded by front-, side- and downward-aimed cameras, with spotlights doing their best to pierce the murky blackness all around it. The sled was about fifty feet above the sea floor.

"Look! There's a chimney," Gordon shouted. "Billy, steady the sled so we can video and measure it. I think it's about forty feet high. I've seen them several times that high but this will definitely do. Finally we can test our new probe right down into the mantle."

Jason, who was standing beside Karen turned and whispered to her. "We've designed what looks like a flexible catheter that we'll insert directly down into the chimney, as far as it'll go. And then for the serious part of this investigation, we'll insert an even smaller probe to hopefully penetrate the molten mass we expect to find."

Karen eyed him. "For a microbiologist, you know an awful lot about this."

"Yup. For several weeks I've been briefed on the details of the experiment, and now that Buddy is out of commission I'll be the one going down to insert the mantle probe. Oh, look!"

The operator continued to edge the sled forward through the murky water until the tower was just fifteen feet away. There in the front monitor was the face of a chimney tower, its odd protuberances creating the image of a high-rise pagoda. It was over ten feet across at the base and tapered slowly upward, marked by a variety of colors and covered with living things, a delicate fuzz of microorganisms, crabs of differing sizes, and tube worms reaching many feet out into the surrounding water.

"Look at that," Billy intoned. "An oasis of heat teaming with life in a cold dark world thousands of feet below the last vestiges of sunlight. Ah, and the height is sixty-five feet."

"That's too high for our probe to get down all the way inside to the mantle."

"We can break it off halfway down," Billy suggested.

Gordon acknowledged the suggestion. "Right. So, a good day! Simson, your equipment is superb! And Pennypacker should be commended, too. Great teamwork! Duke, my hat's off to you and your crew. I'm just thrilled. And now for the next steps. Perhaps even some unscheduled surprises will be in store."

After dinner, Jason asked Karen to step outside with him for some fresh air. She eagerly responded, and they found a quiet place under the stars to settle and talk.

After a mutually silent moment, he said, "Gordon has asked me to talk over a few things with you."

"Oh." she said without expressing any curiosity, sounding rather disappointed that he didn't have more personal, maybe even romantic things on his mind other than work.

He grinned at her. "Hey," he said. "I wish we had more time for, well, for ourselves. But things are moving fast on this ship, and he wants you updated."

"Well then, carry on sailor."

"Besides, I've hated deceiving you."

"Oh boy, this sounds serious."

"Yes," he replied soberly, "and I think you're going to want to hear this."

"Gordon already alerted me when we were still in San Diego that something was up. He had me promise to say nothing even about the general theme he raised."

"Which was?"

She inhaled deeply, exhaled slowly. "Just that the issue of deep-sea mining is explosive, and this cruise is somehow related."

"Ah, so he did mention it."

"And so what is 'it'? Are we perhaps secretly out here digging up nickel potatoes for the black market?"

"You do have a good imagination. And yes, you're actually slightly on target."

"Out with it. I'm all ears."

"No you're not. You're so much more. But later with that. Here's the scoop. I'll just lay it on you."

"Please."

"Well," he began, "My uncle is in government. And he was in the same class at Princeton with Gordon."

"Oh?"

"Also with the Captain – roommates. They go way back. That's partly why they're together on this ship."

"The plot thickens."

"Karen, this is serious."

"Sorry. And so how do you fit into that triangle of old buddies?"

"For starters I'm a bit beyond my PhD. I'm twenty-seven, on board this ship to help Gordon accomplish something of vital importance."

"Vital importance to whom?"

"Perhaps the whole planet. Certainly the wellbeing of all creatures below us in this vast ocean – in all oceans."

"And so we're back to mining," she guessed.

"Exactly. On one side are people like Gordon desperately looking for alternatives to crude strip mining. And on the other side of the equation there are the mining corporations and other get-rich players who want to rape and pillage the ocean floor and to hell with ecological concerns and fair equity of the ocean's wealth."

"Yes, I get all that."

"My, you're impatient tonight."

"Maybe I'm not pleased that it took so long for you and me to have this conversation. I want you to be honest with me."

"Well damnit, that's what I'm trying to do."

They fell silent, side by side but miles apart.

"Sorry," she finally said. "That wasn't fair. I just thought that we had no secrets between us."

"I hope you understand that I have a very firm agreement with Gordon, and with others also. I had to get their okay before talking with you."

"Ah. So. Okay then – out with it. What are we really up to on this big houseboat?"

"First of all I don't mean to demean the research formally stated for this voyage. Science urgently wants to know what we'll find in our deep-mantle probe. But the sled and sub are also both armed for some extracurricular activities."

"So that means," she quickly concluded, "that the designer of the sub and sled also knows what's up."

"Yes. Of necessity. We've been working on this for almost a year now."

"And what exactly are the sub and sled armed to accomplish?"

"We're going to go down and experiment with two opposing approaches to mining and demonstrate the environmental effects of each."

"Ah. I see. And you'll report to whom with those findings?"

He hesitated. "Honestly I don't know the answer to that, but I do know that major regulation decisions at both national and international levels will be impacted by what we might accomplish here in the next few weeks, assuming nothing goes wrong.

"In addition to the stated mission to explore the bottom, Aaron will be using the sled to retrieve the mineral nodules. My job is to record the outcomes. I guess that also means watching others aboard for their interference. Aaron has done consulting work for mining companies. I think I know where he stands. Captain Pearson appears to be willing to do whatever pleases his superiors at Frontier Explorers, and their role in all of this is at least unknown to me."

"And why exactly are you telling me this? And really, why did Professor Blake want me on this ship in the first place?"

Jason grinned. "Maybe I asked him to bring you onboard."

"What?"

"Just kidding."

- 7 -

The Accident

~~~~~~~~~~~~~~~~

Karen didn't get up before dawn. Her alarm went off at 6:15 and for the first time on board, she awoke without wondering where she was. In fact she realized she was beginning to like life at sea and regretted there wasn't more time to do everything she wanted to each day. Definitely again today she wanted to join Pennypacker and his handling crew as they prepared the launch.

Her reverie was broken by a light knock on her door. It was Jason, shouting through the door. "Want to have breakfast with me?"

Right then Karen felt rather than heard the rumble of the launch winch. "Better still," she shouted back, "let's get on the flight deck and watch the launch."

Taking the flight of stairs up to the 02 level, they found the flight deck bathed in brilliant sunlight. The sea was so calm the sun reflected off its oily surface. Jason pointed to the now-vertical A-frame and estimated that the sled would be in the water in ten minutes. As they stood in the middle of the helo pad, shading their eyes, the sled emerged from the aft deck, being lifted very slowly into their view.

Karen had not yet quite appreciated the unique machine's size, complexity, and probable cost – another grand effort to expand humankind's ever-widening horizons. This too is a space shot, she thought, but without the dramatic blast of smoke and media coverage. Whoever had envisioned this new probe machine ought to be highly congratulated. It was a true scientific monster.

The sound of a shot rang out aft. They both jumped. Karen flinched and reflexively ducked, hunching her shoulders. Jason's head jerked around toward the noise, looking fearfully for the source of the gunfire. And at the same time they both saw the sled pivot into the starboard stanchion of the A-frame. One of the two mechanical arms collapsed. The sled was left hanging by the remaining halyard at a precarious 45-degree angle.

Aladdin vibrated with the impact. Everyone aboard knew instantly that something was seriously wrong, and over the loudspeakers Pennypacker's voice blared:

"Clear the deck! Clear the deck! Get away from the sled. Take cover inside!"

Getting the sled back on deck now became imperative. The single thick support wire was designed to bear all the weight, but that certainly wasn't something to count on.

Captain Pearson and Doctor Kline appeared on the starboard deck among the handling crew. Pennypacker approached them on the run. "Captain, I've got this. I'll coach the winch operator. The sled is suspended over the sub so first we need to pivot the A-frame forward, then lower the sled to a foot over its cradle. I'll need every available hand to haul it into position."

Duke rose to the occasion. "Just tell me what you need. I'll be on the bridge."

Pennypacker headed aft, running fast while using his cell phone to communicate with the winch operator. Karen and Jason watched silently.

Ten minutes later the sled was being successfully secured in its cradle. The Captain asked Gordon, Aaron, Simson and Jason to his cabin. Charlie was included in case there was any urgent communication required. Duke sat down in one of the chairs around the table and gestured for the others to join him. Making an effort to appear undaunted by the accident, he looked spooked nonetheless, and he spoke without his usual vitality.

"Damn. What the hell went wrong!"

Simson spoke up immediately. "Aft cable snapped. Sounded like a rifle report, did you hear it? Sounded worse that it is. Doesn't look like anything serious. We have two extra cables. We can get it repaired in twenty-four hours, just lose one day.

The Captain spoke up. "Get me quick assessment of damage right now."

"Pennypacker is busy securing the sled, but he knows we're awaiting his report."

Aaron was still shaken. "I'm damn tired of one accident after another. We've got to get our research out here done."

Gordon spoke softly. "If the launch can be green-lighted by dawn, down we go tomorrow. Duke, talk to me."

The Captain hesitated. "It could have been simply a random accident. But what if it wasn't? Too many accidents. I run a clean ship. I'm not used to accidents of any kind under my watch. But I agree, we need to push forward ... regardless."

Gordon looked at him closely. "So I'm wondering, do we want to deploy the manned sub or the sled tomorrow?"

Simson spoke up. "I think both options are available. The port camera still isn't repaired, but I'll make every effort to have the Bird set for tomorrow morning." He turned to the Captain. "Do you want to send it down if it isn't entirely one hundred percent?"

"Well that's a hard call."

Gordon bristled. "We can't wait if it's just a tiny risk. You all know as well as I do that this charter is over in a month."

"There are going to be a lot of questions when we get back to port," the Captain said, "but we know the stakes here. We've got to get the job done."

Gordon turned to the communications officer. "Charlie, please return to Communications and alert us if there's any incoming traffic. Thank you."

Charlie looked rather hurt by being so summarily dismissed, but he rose and departed at once.

"Okay then, let's get down to it now," the Captain said gruffly to the four other men. "We are definitely experiencing more than our share of difficulties on this mission. Especially the last two, the sub yesterday, and now this. I can't remember a properly maintained cable ever failing. I'd say we've got a very serious problem on board. To be blunt, I think we're being sabotaged."

Simson reacted without any consideration of who he was talking to. "Preposterous! There are logical explanations for everything. We just don't know yet what they all are. You are being paranoid."

Gordon looked deeply conflicted. "Well we were wondering earlier if someone might have removed the buoys from the sled to undermine our research. And somebody might have slashed the rubber sealant on the sub latch. And then of course the whole Bird episode down there. But we had a great day yesterday. If this is the work of sabotage, who would put human lives at stake just to stop our research?"

The Captain grumbled impatiently. "Come on, are you unwilling to even consider the possibility? I have the responsibility of this whole ship! I'm telling you all right now. To hell with ecology if my ship is in danger. If one other thing happens, I will terminate this contract. You can find somebody else to finish your precious project."

"Jason," Gordon said to the youngest man at the table, "you've been with this project from the start. We don't know for sure if it's safe to make another dive, until we can determine the truth. What's your read? You're the one set to go down and do the deep stuff tomorrow. Are you game?"

"And remember," Duke interrupted, "there was the crane that almost dropped all the project computers on the pier before we sailed, not to mention the brakes failing on the truck hauling the sled to the pier in March. And the intermittent gyro failure on the Bird, and the software glitch ... does that all add up to proof of sabotage?"

They fell silent, awaiting Jason's response.

"For me," he finally said very quietly, "I'm totally dedicated to getting our primary study completed and into the right hands within the next month. Go down, run the mining-technique tests, get all the video data and so forth processed, write the paper and hand it over. Get down there and demonstrate what strip mining will do to the ocean floor. We must accomplish this now and not later, regardless of any risks involved. But at the same time, whoever's screwing with us, let's find him!"

"Good boy, yes," from Gordon. "Press on, *and* start an investigation. The bottom-line first question is, if there's a traitor among us, who can we really definitely trust?"

The room fell silent. All four men looked at each other without saying another word.

Later that day, Jason and Karen were out on deck at their favorite retreat spot. Jason had been told by the Professor to update her, and now she was sitting silently, staring out over the vastness of the sea they were trying to save from devastation. She finally turned her head and looked into Jason's soft blue eyes which were sparkling with determination.

"No," she said emphatically. "I can't let you go down and risk your life – not for anything."

He took in her words, and then smiled slightly. "I don't know why, but I'm happy to hear you say that. And I'm sorry to override you, but there's no question in my mind. I'm going down tomorrow. We're doing this."

She held his gaze and held her breath at the same time. Then she exhaled with a loud impatient huff. "You are a stubborn man, you know that."

"Only when it really matters," he replied evenly. "Otherwise I think I'm fairly accommodating."

"I don't think I could bear to watch you and the sub disappear down into the depths."

"So please just don't be on deck tomorrow. In fact Gordon asked me if you could start looking for anything or anyone who might seem suspicious. He says your intuition is spot-on. Without raising any eyebrows, start sniffing."

"Like a dog?"

"Like a sleuth."

"Ah. Well I can do that. Better than watching you plunge into the depths with a saboteur at large. So do you have any initial suspicions? Who knows what you're really studying on this voyage, and are there any of those you and the Professor don't really trust?"

"Gordon offered to set up a conference call with the higher-ups of the covert side of our research project, tell them what's happening, get their feedback; but he wants to get down and gather the data before the call."

"So tell me now, who on board actually knows of the mining tests?"

"Besides Gordon, Aaron, of course, the Captain, Simson, and me – and now you – no one knows. And no one else knows of our suspicions. Gordon asked the communications guy, I forget his name, to exit the room when we started talking sabotage."

"But surely," Karen pushed, "if the sled was redesigned at Simson's factory to include the sea-floor mining feature ..."

"Of course we talked all that through," Jason interrupted. "Obviously a few engineers and such back at the sub factory who worked on the sled modifications might have suspected something. But that's a long shot according to Simson. He personally hired his team and can vouch for them. Besides, it's gotta be someone on board this vessel, and the Captain assures us he kept a tight eye on all that."

"Well what about the sub operators, Buddy and Derek – and also Pennypacker, he must know too."

"Right, but they just know the overt basics, that we're going to run some mining-tech tests."

"So, whom do we trust? Who can we eliminate?"

Jason hesitated. "Karen, you're asking all the right questions, I can see you're good at this. Top of the list is Captain Pearson. Gordon and I conferred just now in private about him. He's a traditional conservative and in general pro-big-business. He's ready to scuttle the cruise if there's any real danger to his ship or crew. Gordon won't question his sincerity about our cause. He loves the ocean."

"Well I would question his sincerity."

"I know you don't like him."

She shrugged. "Tough to like a misogynist."

Jason ignored that. "Frankly I don't think we'll ever get convincing evidence regarding the sabotage to date. But keep your eyes open for anything that seems off, especially in the launch team. You've been hanging around them on deck. Make your presence felt tomorrow morning, will you?"

"How can I do that if I'm below deck mourning your possible demise?"

He smiled and then got serious. "Get tough. Be out there early tomorrow morning. And if you can, hang out with the crew during dinner and so forth. This is important. And hey, I'm not going to die down there, I can feel it."

She reached over and put her hand on his knee. "Okay, I'll be positive."

"And meanwhile we're busy considering suspicious bad guys. If we can isolate likely suspects to watch, we'll transfer them to other jobs or even send them ashore."

"So is that it? Anything else?" she pushed, removing her hand from his knee.

"We're building a list of who had access to the submersibles. They sit on deck where anyone can get to them. A saboteur could do a lot of damage with a knife or hammer. We're posting a guard starting right now."

"Good."

"And we'll have someone get started examining the records of everyone on board. Plus Simson trusts Pennypacker to help. We'll also bring in the communications guy. I can have him handle all the sensitive-message traffic."

"So," she said. "Roll the cameras – action!"

"I think Gordon wants you to ease up on your various intern assignments to focus on this instead."

"I gotta run. Oh, there was a dream I had last night. You and I were way off somewhere on vacation. It was just delightful."

- 8 -

New Research

~~~~~~~~~~~~~~~~

The Captain was sitting in his stateroom mulling over what he needed to do first when Pennypacker and Charlie burst in.

"Bad news," Pennypacker blurted, obviously angry. "That cable was rotten. The central strands were rusty and broken. I've already sent a message back to our office to get them to pull the shipyard records, but my guess is the usual stress tests weren't run."

"So who's at fault on that?" the Captain demanded.

"Maybe I should have checked this personally," Pennypacker admitted, "but we've had nothing but outstanding support from that team in the past."

"We're damn lucky only one cable parted when it did. The sled was suspended over the Bird!"

"I've got my team examining the other halyard and all the spare wires. If they're okay I'll rewind the winch and we'll be back in business."

"Alright. Proceed unless you hear from me or Gordon. Charlie, this is a very sensitive issue. I want you to treat everything top-secret on all new incoming or outgoing communications. Bring such documents immediately to my desk – understood?

"Cutting to the chase, we suspect we might have a saboteur on board. I need you two to join our investigation team."

An hour later the ship's phone rang in Gordon's stateroom. "Professor, this is Charlie down in Communications. Your office says they will start sending data on employees late this afternoon. They're putting staff on overtime as you requested. Sounds like they're taking this every bit as seriously as we are."

"Assuming there's no plant in the office who could alter the data being sent to us. Thanks, Charlie." Gordon immediately regretted expressing any hint of his paranoia.

Sitting on his lower bunk bed, Karen waited a bit impatiently while Jason left his cabin to retrieve the daily log down in the Control Room. Perhaps there would be some information in the log to set them on course. Shortly after his departure she stood up to stretch and casually examine her surroundings. She was consumed by curiosity to find out more about this man. Glancing at his desk, she noticed an opened envelope addressed to Jason Crocker in feminine handwriting.

There was a photograph sticking out slightly from the envelope, and she couldn't resist the temptation to pull it out. The picture revealed a blonde about her age dressed in short shorts and a halter-top, leaning casually against an old automobile. It almost looked like a mimic of an advertisement for used cars, but the background showed a driveway in need of weeding, and the corner of a house.

Karen was ambushed by the urge to pull out the letter. She lifted two folded sheets from the envelope and in doing so dropped a 3x5 card on the deck. Ignoring it, she started reading quickly. There were words of affection and loneliness wrapped in mundane news. Jason was clearly missed. The author referred to the photograph as a way for him to remember her. It was signed, "Love, Michele."

Feeling embarrassed and foolish, she started to shove the letter back inside the envelope. She was also suddenly feeling jealous and unreasonably angry. After all, Jason had given her no indication that she was more than a shipboard colleague. Why should she have assumed that he might have a romantic interest in her? Her sinking heart told her clearly something she had not wanted to hear. She was almost certainly falling in love with him.

Once the letter was out of sight, Karen bent over to pick up the card to stuff it in the envelope, too. She found the card had just a few words, "Your sister isn't the only one who misses you. Love, Mom and Dad"

Jason returned to his stateroom with the watch log under his arm. Billy had asked where he was going with it but appeared satisfied with Jason's off-hand remark about needing to pull dates and times on the last two dives. He was surprised to find Karen leaning against the doorframe in the passageway. He had no idea why she was now looking so smug.

"This might tell us something," he said, settling eagerly in the chair at his small desk and immediately beginning to turn pages. Karen took her place on his bunk, legs dangling. Now that she had seen the letter, she looked at Jason in a promising new light.

Time went by while Jason impatiently flipped through the pages. Then he slapped the logbook shut. "Damn. Nothing in the least bit suspicious."

Someone pounded on the door. In walked the Professor. "Oh," he said, surprised. "Am I disturbing anything? I can come back later."

"Come on in," Jason said in his usual friendly voice. "We were just looking over the log. Nothing there."

Without acknowledging Jason's observation, he announced, "I have a bit of serious news."

"What's going on?" Jason asked apprehensively. Karen said not a word.

"Well, we ran down the formal police report on the truck that lost its brakes while transporting the sled. There was partial evidence that someone had tampered with the hydraulic line, so probably there was someone on the mainland indeed wanting to disrupt our research. That's bad news, but it means the saboteur was on the mainland. We still have no concrete evidence that the accidents on board here were anything other than accidents. So Jason, we're thinking about greenlighting tomorrow's dive if you're still game?"

"I think so," Jason replied, and turned to open his laptop. "First, let me get you up to date. I've just briefly looked at each of the five major accidents, as we're still calling them, and I've come up with a list of names of possible suspects. For example, the winch failure could easily have been the work of Pennypacker or anyone on his crew. There are five people on that list."

"But couldn't someone else have done the mischief?" Gordon asked.

"Yeah, that's the problem. If we're looking for just one saboteur, they might have particular skills in that regard, but most likely they wouldn't have the skills to be the suspect in *all* the accidents, including electronics and computers."

"Okay, so that's already several possibilities. Are there any more?"

"Well the next grouping includes people like Buddy and our three PhD watch supervisors, Billy, Julian, and Carl. They appear in virtually every on-board scenario because of their assigned responsibilities. Any watch supervisor could have had access to the submersibles and support equipment and software, before or during their rotation in the monitoring room. And there may be others. Willy Harlow, the winch operator, has been on deck whenever we've done a launch or recovery."

"Alright then," Gordon said tersely, "so I get the point. But does that mean you will or won't dive tomorrow? We still don't have any definite sabotage data one way or the other."

"There's more," Jason said, ignoring the question. "The second accident gives us a similar list of suspects. All have the same ability to access the system, but that accident or whatever was more sophisticated because electronics were involved. I'm also looking into Buddy. I know you trust him, but he's someone who could have done so much mischief, so he's high on my list."

"No!" Gordon moaned. "No, Jason. No."

"Whatever," Jason went on calmly. "My point is, we have loads of hazy suspects but no actual proof of mischief on board. Therefore I am volunteering to be hopeful and positive and take the dive tomorrow. End of story."

Karen reacted. "Aw, Jason, please ..."

He raised his hand to silence her. "Karen, this isn't your decision. The stakes are too high. I'm going down."

"Well if Buddy might be the saboteur," Gordon spoke up again, "I recommend that we take him up on his offer, bruised ribs or not, and have him be the pilot who takes you down."

"You're reading my thoughts." Jason said. "If Buddy *is* the saboteur, he won't harm the sub if he's riding in it. Checkmate – we get our data."

Gordon was notified by Charlie that he's received 39 pages from the mainland office containing 17 employee files. The Professor asked him to call Aaron and Jason for a meeting to begin reviewing the records.

As if by mutual agreement, Karen joined Jason over coffee in the mess. "I still say," she said to him with, her voice terse, "that it's simply too risky to go down tomorrow."

"Karen, I'm someone who takes risks. Get used to it. I have this rare opportunity to finally visit the ocean floor. Do you have any idea how many people would kill to be in my shoes? And Yellow Bird is an exceptional submarine, I feel confident it'll all go well."

"You and the Professor amaze me. We most likely have someone on board actively trying to sabotage this project, and you're going to make a dive down to at least ten thousand feet in a prototype submarine. I think you and the others are letting expediency and ambition overtake common sense."

"Karen, you're being overly pessimistic. Gordon and I talked things through with Simson. He's going to beef up launch security. I trust him entirely."

She slowly shook her head, settling back in her chair. Jason couldn't help admiring how she looked. "I signed up for a simple summer research project," she muttered, "and here I am, right in the middle of a floating melodrama! And look at you, sitting there laughing at my worries, pleased as punch to be putting your life in jeopardy. You're an idiot, Jason Crocker.

This isn't research; it's a crapshoot. Well good luck. I hope it's not a one-way trip to the bottom!"

She pushed her chair back almost violently and stood up. Several people looked over at them. Jason was speechless as she flung her napkin down on the table and stalked away.

Motivated in part by her concern for Jason and the risks implicit in the coming dive, she walked with quick steps aft to view the submarine being prepared for the dive; but before she even got there, Pennypacker shouted at her.

"Karen, wait! You can't go aft today. That rope barrier is a sailor's way of saying 'Keep Out.'" He smiled ruefully. "Simson's orders. Buddy and Derek are the only ones allowed without Simson's permission. They've also locked the door to the winch room, and mounted security cameras to cover the main deck approaches. They're quite serious."

Still upset by his argument with Karen, Jason took his laptop to the Professor's stateroom and joined Gordon and Aaron as they settled around the small table, opening their laptops and beginning to read through all the employee files looking for – what?

It didn't take long for them to realize that they were dealing with more questionable people than they had anticipated. Screening files simply produced a long list of mostly improbable suspects. Gordon was not pleased. "We have targeted over a third of our junior people so far."

They continued to sort through the files in silence. The Chief Scientist was reviewing Bill McCullough's background file when something in his posture distracted Jason. "What's wrong?"

"This doesn't make any sense," Aaron complained. "The record must be incorrect."

Gordon looked up from his reading. "What do you mean?"

"According to this," Aaron said, "Billy worked for Deep Ocean Research just before reporting to *Aladdin*. They competed aggressively for this project. Frontier Explorers edged them out, but there was bad blood. If Billy worked for them, I'm certain he wouldn't be offered a position on this ship."

Gordon muttered, "Well I can personally vouch for Billy. He is *not* our saboteur."

"You seem awfully sure."

Gordon hesitated way too long. "That's because I personally recommended him to Frontier Explorers. I thought you might accuse me of nepotism, so I kept it to myself. He's actually my son-in-law."

"Oh. I see, Well then. Take him off the list. And really, are we wasting time with this? We're facing a very weird conspiracy, and I for one don't know where we go from here."

As the meeting broke up, for Jason the good news was that he could now concentrate on his preparations for the dive. And those preparations included finding Karen. He finally spied her on the forecastle, leaning over the port rail watching the bow wave curl and break into foam. She seemed mesmerized by the flow of water.

As he approached from the side he saw that her lips were just slightly parted. He could see her long eyelashes and pixie nose in profile. He smiled because he thought her nose was cute and that him thinking that thought would probably make her angry. He stood fifteen feet away, wondering what she was thinking.

She must have felt his gaze because there appeared a flicker of awareness in her eyes and then a small smile compressed her lips. Without turning her head she said: "Don't you just hate it when you feel that someone is staring at you?" She pivoted on her heel. "So did the Mounties get their man?"

Jason was relieved by her unexpected playfulness, but the question highlighted the failure of the day. He felt uncomfortable because of what he had to tell her. She misread him and launched into an apology. "Jason, I'm so sorry. I have no idea why I unloaded on you like I did over coffee." She corrected herself: "Actually, I do; but I'm still sorry."

He came up fairly close at her side. "Well if it was you going down," he confessed, "I'd probably be saying the same thing – play it safe, girl. You're too precious, don't do that dive. And darn it all, we didn't find anything in the employee files to give us even a clue as to who a possible saboteur on board might be. Gordon feels demoralized. If you can think of anything you can do for him, don't hesitate to get involved."

"Get involved?" she reacted. "Jason, I am involved. I have been involved. And for what it is worth, I care deeply about the outcome of this cruise. But I mostly care what happens to you. The best thing I could do would be to persuade somebody to cancel tomorrow's dive."

He studied her earnest expression. "That isn't going to happen – but really, I appreciate more than you can imagine your concern about me. You really do boost my spirits."

She smiled wanly. "And who is going to lift my spirits as I watch you make the descent in the morning?"

Jason wanted to put his arms around her, and he hoped she wouldn't mind; but they were standing just twenty feet in front of the bridge. He assumed that behind those mirror-like windows several people were watching them.

After dinner Gordon asked Duke, Aaron, and Simson to do a run-through of the dive with Buddy and Jason. They went into a conference room and talked things through, considering whether or not to include two additional passengers to fill each seat. They decided against it without voicing any pessimistic reasons. The evening rehearsal was standard procedure but Jason noticed that Gordon's eyes kept examining Buddy as Aaron reviewed preparations that had taken place over the course of the day.

Jason wanted to blurt out and say: "You guys are so obvious. Why don't you just shout your accusations at Buddy and let him defend himself?" But he kept his mouth shut and they continued, scheduling the dive for nine o'clock sharp in the morning. Once in the water, they decided the sub was to get down to the tower as fast as possible, knock off its top and insert the deep probe. It would be an ambitious and hopefully scientifically rewarding achievement.

"Jason," Gordon said as they were departing the conference room, "before you turn in you should go get your laptop, you left it in my stateroom earlier. Take care of it. You've recorded a lot of sensitive and important data."

"I'll retrieve my homework. Thanks."

Blake handed him the key to the room, and that was that.

But that wasn't quite all to the story of the forgotten laptop because someone else also had the intent of entering the Professor's stateroom. While the rehearsal meeting was taking place, it was a perfect opportunity for someone to visit the stateroom where Gordon and the others had spent much of the day reviewing employee records. A quick-moving shadow of a man worked the stateroom lock, and quite quickly gained entrance. Slipping inside, he closed and locked the door behind him.

A quick search was made in the semi-darkness, but other than the laptop which sat quite visibly on the gently swaying table, there wasn't a shred of paper or other evidence left in the room. The silent shadowy figure completed the search and then came to a pause, looking at the laptop. Anyone stupid enough to leave it unattended where it could slip off a flat surface might also be stupid enough to leave a flash drive in it. Ah, look at that! Good hunting!

Suddenly the man froze. Loud footsteps were heard descending the stairwell adjacent to the stateroom. The dark figure moved into the closet several feet from the door and waited. A knife shown slightly as it was pulled out of its sheath in readiness.

Jason took the key Gordon had given him and stuck it in the lock, turned it and then entered the room, suspecting nothing. He looked tired. This was the first time he had been alone since waking, and he realized how exhausted he was. He flipped on the overhead light, turned, and looked around the room, numb to any vague instinct that he wasn't alone.

The laptop was sitting on the tabletop where he'd left it. He flipped up the screen briefly and then closed it with a click. Then he remembered the flash drive. He looked at the back of the laptop to discover that it was missing.

He stood there a moment looking around with more focused attention at the room. The flash drive wasn't anywhere else to be found. But he was sure it had been in the laptop. So where was it now? He walked around the room, looking more closely. He even paused to open the closet door, but then, feeling tired and impatient to be in bed, he turned away from the closet and the knife awaiting him. He left the room, flipping off the overhead light as he departed.

The vague presence in the closet stepped out and sheathed the knife. "What a bloody fool," the man said with disdain, and made his own exit.

- 9 -
Jason's Dive
~~~~~~~~~~~~~~~~

Karen had not been able to sleep. She was convinced that, after the string of so-called accidents the project had experienced, a few basic security measures and a tentative identification of a possible saboteur would be insufficient assurance of a safe dive. She had turned in early simply to be alone, but she couldn't bear the bleak isolation and so decided to look for casual company on the mess deck.

No such luck. It was late and no one was around to chat with. So she wandered up to the monitoring room and found a handful of people there but no one she knew. Her sense of anxiety and depression seemed to grow rather than dissipate outside her stateroom. The entire ship felt ominous this time of night. She could almost palpably sense the presence on board of someone who wished to do further harm to – to whom? And with what motive?

Staring into the blackness of the ocean night, she tried to convince herself that she was being paranoid. She tried to convince herself that she wasn't in love with the man set to descend over ten thousand feet into the void tomorrow. Failing in both attempts, she turned on her heel and walked quickly inside, down all those scary passageways, back into her room.

In bed with the lights off, she curled into a fetal position to sleep, but that was out of the question. She tossed and turned fitfully, with images of the Bird deep down losing communication and power and settling irretrievably on the ocean floor while its two passengers slowly ran out of air.

She sat up in bed gasping. She sucked in air and tried to push away the nightmare, realizing she was obsessing with – what? The very thought of Jason willingly dropping his youthful body down into the sub tomorrow and sinking in that metallic coffin down and away from her was agonizing. Would she even have the nerve to be on deck to watch?

Ah, she admitted finally to herself, perhaps there was still magic in the world. Perhaps she'd somehow in such a short time already let this amazing guy into her life and heart. But now? Was having to suffer through a terrifying nightmare really a required part of falling in love? And hey, more realistically, what might she do tomorrow to make sure a disaster didn't occur?

She finally fell asleep while running one person after another on board through her mind, urgently trying to determine which one was the saboteur, because, yes, she now felt intuitively afraid that there was evil on board this ship. She knew that sounded like an overused cliché. Her rational mind scolded her for being foolishly, childishly melodramatic. Accidents after all did tend to come in clusters. She'd studied that in her statistics course last semester. That seemed like ages ago. Her gut still warned her that there was a malevolent presence on board.

Jason woke up before his alarm clock went off. He felt hot and sweaty, but he knew he wasn't afraid of the dive. In fact he thrived on taking risks and making it through a challenge. What he admitted to himself he feared most was that if an emergency occurred, he wouldn't handle himself well. His mind coughed up memories of his father shouting at him when he was little, telling him he just wasn't up to snuff every time he failed at something. In his hopelessly floundering early-morning imagination he saw Karen also laughing at him, scorning him, rejecting him because he was a failure.

He slept fitfully, and made it topside two hours later feeling the opposite of rested. The weather had been picture-perfect for diving operations throughout the week, but this morning the sky was mostly overcast with just a vague rust-colored sunrise. Long swells foretold worsening weather even though the local forecast still predicted acceptable parameters for the recovery at the end of the day.

Jason made his way to a cup of coffee before he and Buddy would participate in the required pre-flight briefing in the monitoring room. His eyes quickly scanned the mess hall for Karen, urgently needing to make contact with her before the dive. She was nowhere to be seen. The launch was going to be an hour later than before for security reasons. No one was to be on deck around the sub before dawn. But where was she? He'd been almost rude to her when she challenged his decision to make the dive. Was she now ignoring him? She'd made herself vulnerable; she'd shown how much she cared for him even after so few days together.

The briefing after breakfast was terse and formal with everyone acting positive and upbeat, hiding any subtle undercurrents of apprehension. Buddy seemed a bit withdrawn and all business. Gordon and Aaron likewise were just going through the motions as they outlined the intentions for the dive and dished out minor last-minute directions. The Captain was his usual grumpy self. Only Simson, who carried much of the strain of the dive on his designer shoulders, seemed overtly concerned and quiet.

Jason eyed all of them, remembering the half-buried glances of mutual suspicion he'd seen in this core group the day before. Were they still harboring lurking suspicious of each other? Jason felt himself suddenly looking at each of them with similar suspicions. Which of them would have hidden motives for undermining this research? Hell, it was impossible to even imagine that, but with such high stakes resting on the results, anything was possible.

Then Jason found himself physically caught up in an inevitable flow as he proceeded aft to walk those fateful steps across the deck and climb up the metal steps to board the sub. He looked sharply at all the various players in this seemingly secure morning maritime procedure.

Everyone looked focused on their jobs. No one stood out at all as a possible suspect. The sub had been monitored all night with surveillance cameras, nothing was amiss – except Jason's stomach's continuing nervous edge. But really, he told himself, he should be enjoying the rush of all this. Come on!

And then there she was, watching the scene unfold from the flight deck with the Professor at her side. Jason waved to her; she waved back. His mood brightened, but they were too far away! He couldn't say anything to her. He'd spent half an hour wandering around the ship earlier, hoping to run into her. He felt his frustration.

And now Derek was assisting Simson with the final visual checks. It was time to duck down into the sub.

A moment later the hatch was being sealed.

The Yellow Bird settled quickly into the Pacific, took a few long swells over the hatch cover, and then disappeared into the dark water. Jason watched Buddy concentrate on getting the sub into proper profile for the descent. He was working smoothly, although he flinched a little when reaching over his head, the ribs still bothering him.

The light faded faster than Jason had expected. The water changed to an ever-darker hue as if someone was turning down the brightness on a screen. There were no signs of marine life. Jason turned his attention again to the interior.

"Being inside the Bird seems so different," he said to Buddy, "without any sunlight beaming in through the hatch."

"Do you feel a bit claustrophobic?" Buddy responded.

"Oh not really. This is just so, well, exciting to actually be down here, and headed down all the way."

They were passing five hundred feet. "Wait till we're down and we turn on the lights," Buddy said. "You'll get an eyeful out the windows and on the videos. Seeing the ocean floor so far down teeming with life is such a rush, but I admit, the idea of living down here at great depth in this total dark is slightly horrifying to me." He grinned. "The bottom is a great place to visit, but I wouldn't want to live down there."

Captain Pearson was on the bridge, and from there he saw Karen mount the ladder and approach his cabin door, which was also visible from his vantage point. He moved from the pilot house to intercept her.

"What are you trying to do?" he grumbled.

"I've got to see Gordon. It's important."

"It's not as important as what he is doing. Come back later."

Karen felt the color rise in her cheeks. "You don't understand," she said. "This is directly related to the dive. I've *got* to see him, right now, and only Gordon is going to tell me to go away."

Duke took a step toward her. She chose to ignore him and turned to knock on the door anyway. But before she could do so, the Captain grabbed her wrist in an unbreakable grip, and used leverage on her arm to spin her back to face him.

"You don't listen very well, do you, girl," he hissed. "You have a choice. Walk away right now or I'll have you carried away."

As Karen started to reply, the door opened from the inside. Gordon stood there and took in the Captain gripping Karen's wrist. "What the hell is going on?"

Karen spoke up instantly. "Gordon, I think we were wrong about Buddy."

Duke reacted to her terse words. "What has Buddy got to do with this?"

Karen paled. She'd assumed the Professor had discussed their suspicions with the Captain. She yanked her arm free from his grip and stepped back. Gordon looked at her sternly. "Karen, take it easy. I'll speak with you in a few minutes. Duke, please – a word."

"What's all this about?"

"I was going to tell you but didn't have a chance yet. Jason and Karen found data that identified Buddy as possibly being our nemesis."

"What? You're investigating one of *my* employees?"

"It appears that Buddy tampered with some files while back on the mainland. Nothing directly related to any of the accidents, but why else would he alter data? That put him high on our suspect list. We're trying to find out if he altered any other information. He could have been actively undermining our efforts all summer, and quite possibly now on board."

Duke sneered, "Gordon, you are a fool. I can't believe that a man with your reputation and intelligence would jump to such conclusions based just on some flimsy paper trail."

"Duke, ease up. This is serious."

"You are darn right it's serious, and if Buddy is a suspect, why the hell did you ask me to put him in the sub today? But never mind. I know for a fact that you are wrong. There's something I haven't told you. I hoped it wouldn't come to this. But I know that Buddy was himself the victim of sabotage – he was a very fortunate survivor of the last dive."

"Go on."

"When we retrieved the sub at the end of the dive, I had Simson go over it very carefully so that I could document any damage attributable to your research and not our mishandling."

"And Simson clearly reported that the sub was unscathed."

"Yes, except for a very minor, or so we assumed, observation that the ballast hooks had been bent. That means that Buddy could not have released most of the ballast weight – and that would mean that the sub would have risen extremely slowly to the surface, or not at all. Derek and Buddy were at risk for their lives.

So obviously Buddy isn't a suspect – unless he's suicidal."

"That doesn't make sense. Buddy and Derek did rise up and breach."

"I think I've figured that out – your mysterious sea monster. We would have lost the sub if it hadn't been rolled over like it was. As best I can tell, the ballast must have settled when the sub was on its back, and then it came off the hooks when the sub continued its somersault."

The two men stared at each other.

"Incredible," Gordon muttered.

"Yeah," Duke agreed. "And if I'm right, and I'd put money on it, that mystery creature actually saved their lives. It's idiotic to think like that, but ..."

Gordon interrupted him. "I wish to hell you had told me this earlier. I pushed to have Buddy pilot this new dive so that he couldn't or wouldn't do any more harm. Now all bets are off. We still have a potential killer on the loose but no idea who he is. Damn. Let's get Buddy and Jason back on board!"

Jason was fascinated with the sparkling marine life outside his view port. "Buddy, you were right. This is fantastic."

"Just like falling through the stars. Make a wish on the brightest one you see. We really don't need power until we start for the surface, but we're using the engine to descend a bit faster."

Jason was relieved that Buddy's last trip to this depth hadn't produced any latent fears. He still had his sense of humor. This guy was all right, Jason found himself thinking. No chance he's the saboteur. But then the thought occurred to him, if Buddy was in the clear, then who had done all those things to sabotage their research?

Karen was right outside the Captain's stateroom door when it burst open. "Out of the way," the Captain ordered her, pushing past. And Professor Blake came rushing out right behind him, leaving Karen to hurry in their wake down to the monitoring room.

"Call the sub!" the Captain ordered as he came into the room. "Tell Buddy to return to the surface! NOW!"

"Julian, do it," Gordon seconded.

Phelps looked back and forth from one to the other. And before he could collect his thoughts and act, someone shouted, "The hologram! The sub has gone into a steep dive! They're headed for the bottom!"

All eyes focused on the hologram display. The yellow nose was aimed down and the sub was accelerating.

Gordon shouted: "What's their current depth? How much water do they have left?"

Aboard the submersible, Jason had just turned to look out the port when he felt the nose plunge. His first reaction was to wonder what Buddy had done, but Buddy was working feverishly to pull back on the stick and regain control. And he was having no success. Too busy to talk, he was desperately trying to sort out what had gone wrong. All Jason could do was watch.

The Bird continued to pitch over. As it passed the vertical, it did exactly what Buddy had told them it would do. It rolled to right itself. Pitching forward and passing through fully vertical, it rolled again, corkscrewing itself into the depths at increasing speed.

The two passengers held on tightly, watching in horror as the depth sensor registered four, then five, then six thousand feet, on their way to the sea floor. They'd dived through three thousand feet of seawater in less than twelve minutes – they were very quickly running out of time before they crashed.

Aboard *Aladdin* people watched the hologram with helpless fascination. There was absolutely nothing they could do as the submarine continued its plunge into the abyss. In a ghoulish effort to be helpful, the display operator kept adjusting the scale so that as the sub neared the bottom, they could see it more clearly. Karen felt like she was watching someone falling off a building, helpless to do anything about it.

And Jason was too frightened to notice the rising nausea in his stomach as the twisting submarine threw him and his companion violently about. The pain was excruciating for Buddy. The first roll had thrown him against the steering console, re-injuring his ribs. Objects that had come loose as the sub continued its plunge also hampered his efforts. There was blood over his right eye where his head had slammed into the bulkhead. He was panting as he attempted to pull the nose up, but the harder he worked at it, the less the sub responded.

"They've got just over two thousand feet to go." Gordon said expressionlessly, watching the gyrating submarine that was minutes away from impact. The sea floor was mostly volcanic rock, but at that speed and angle it didn't matter what the bottom was. The sub would implode at the moment of collision. The passengers would mercifully perish almost instantly.

"Buddy, let go! Let go! Let go of the stick!" Jason was pulling at straws. Panic and the certainty that their lives were over if they hit at this approach made him grab at a drastic possibility. "Stop pulling on the stick!"

Buddy was now resigned to his fate, and that may have been the sole reason he complied with Jason's order. With a sigh that sounded like a death rattle, he raised his hands off the controls and gripped his seat in anticipation of the next roll. It would likely be their last.

Without Buddy's efforts to pull the stick aft, the nose now started to rise slowly. Jason was the first to notice his center of gravity settling back into his seat. He glanced at the pressure sensor and saw 11,412 feet, the descent numbers still rising but now more slowly. Their rate of descent was decreasing: 600 feet, 525 feet, 475 feet. They were still descending rapidly, but the submarine's attitude was no longer precarious. The Bird was leveling!

Buddy was sprawled in his seat in too much pain to notice. The blood on his forehead was not the result of a serious cut, but it had seeped into the socket, shutting his right eye. Jason feared that Buddy would make an impulsive attempt to pull back on the stick, so he rolled out of his chair onto his knees next to the injured man and reached across his chest to protect the controls. Buddy merely stared at him with his left eye, breathing heavily. Jason merely stared back. He felt totally in shock, but he also now had new hope that they might survive.

At 11,650 feet Jason feared they were still going to impact the bottom at a rate that would break the sub open like an egg. So he did the only thing they hadn't tried. If he was wrong, it would all be over in less than a minute. Gripping the stick, he jammed it forward, with all his senses tuned into the movement of the sub.

At first it seemed that his action wasn't having any effect. Because of his awkward position, using one arm to fend off any attempts by his fellow passenger to grab the stick while using his free hand to manipulate the controls, he couldn't get a look at the panel to observe the submarine's dive angle. The figures on the depth sensor rolled from 11,745 to 11,910. They were less than one thousand feet from the bottom. Jason knew all too well that the sea floor, like terrain anywhere else on the Earth's surface, was not flat. They could impact the rock bed at any second now, or they might descend into a fissure, buying them a bit of time but ultimately putting them into a position from which they could not be recovered.

Aboard *Aladdin* the hologram had become intermittent. At one point there was a collective groan from the onlookers as the submarine had just disappeared. Someone muttered an expletive, conceding defeat. But then the submersible reappeared, clearly having gained some depth under its tiny hull.

Karen heard Phelps say: "Wow – yes!"

Gordon took the underwater telephone and called the submarine. "Buddy. Jason. This is Gordon. Can you hear me?"

There was no response. They waited.

"Buddy. Jason. Key your mike if you cannot speak. Can you hear me?"

The recent recovery from certain death was now being overtaken in Gordon's mind by new urgent questions. What or who had caused the submarine to plunge out of control? What on Earth was going on down there?

"Gordon, this is Jason. I couldn't find the mike. We hear you."

Karen, who had been weeping out of sheer panic, now wept out of sheer relief at hearing Jason's voice. He was alright; the sub was alright. Get him back up. She realized that she was an emotional mess, but no one was paying the least bit of attention to her.

The Captain grabbed the mike now: "Jason, are you alright? Is Buddy alright? What is your status?"

"The submarine's controls ..." He stopped and started again, *"Buddy has re-injured his ribs and has a cut over his right eye. Right now he seems half-conscious, but he'll live. I am unhurt. The sub's controls are not working properly – I think the signals are reversed. When I tried to push the stick forward to signal a dive, the nose came up. That's how I stopped the downward spiral. We are now over the bottom at one hundred fifty-three feet."*

"Jason, as soon as you and Buddy can figure out how to bring the sub to the surface safely, do it. The dive is aborted. I repeat. The dive is aborted."

"I acknowledge. Dive aborted. Give me a few minutes to assess our condition."

- 10 -

Hostages

~~~~~~~~~~~~~~~~

Jason just sat there for a very long moment. Someone had done something to the sub, and there were possibly other deadly tricks coming any moment. Someone topside could be observing the present situation and activating Plan B to keep the sub down for the count. All Jason had to do was second-guess and avert Plan B and, of course, with or without Buddy's help, manage to get the sub headed upward.

The engine died.

Jason was not at first aware that the sub was no longer moving through the water, but as it slowed and did not respond to the stick, he was confronted with the reality that this might be the end. He fought to control his panic.

"Buddy, come on, you've got to focus," Jason said urgently to his limp companion. "The pain isn't going to kill you, but if we don't regain control of this sub and head up, we're definitely going to die. Do you hear me?"

But Buddy just sat there in a daze, staring vaguely straight ahead with his one good eye. It was becoming clear to Jason that his dive partner was suffering from more than a minor cut over his right eye. Jason felt highly frustrated, and consumed by a growing claustrophobic fear.

"Buddy, I need your help! How do I start the engine?"

No response from the operator. They were now motionless, suspended just above the seabed. For no reason, Jason remembered the definition of limbo from his catechism class: a place or state of confinement, of neglect ... or oblivion. They were definitely in limbo. And Jason was the only one who could get them out. He thought for the first time of Karen up above. This must be pure hell for her too.

"Control, this is Jason."

*"*Yes – and what can we do for you?"

"Buddy is not responding. I need advice about how to operate this thing."

Simson was already in the monitoring room. In anticipation of the question, he had been poring over prints of the sub's circuitry and hydraulics. Julian was trying to locate Derek. Gordon thought it bitterly ironic that not only was Buddy exonerated, but now they must rely on others who may in fact want to subvert their rescue efforts. Could Derek be trusted? Where was he?

"Jason, this is Simson. You are not in immediate danger. The sub has self-adjusting ballast that heats and cools to keep you stable at your ordered depth."

"But – how do I start the propulsion system?"

Simson walked Jason through the simple steps to get the propellers turning. With movement, Jason felt more in control. To ascend, the computer on board would disable the self-adjusting ballast, but Jason would also have to jettison some of the weights.

"Jason, you are beginning to break up on the telephone, and the signal is getting weak on the hologram. You are moving out of range."

"Roger. I am going to try to turn the sub around, but I don't trust the controls. Let me experiment."

Jason put down the telephone and grasped the stick in front of Buddy. He put gentle pressure on it, moving it slightly to the right to turn to starboard. His eyes were fixed on the gyrocompass on the instrument panel, and the compass confirmed his suspicions. The submarine was turning left, not right.

"Simson, how much weight should I release?"

"Try jettisoning just one bank. You ought to start seeing new readings on your depth gauges. It will be slow. We'll take this one step at a time. Give the sub more power and start to gently climb."

"Roger – applying power."

Jason gingerly edged the stick forward – and the submarine slowly began to accelerate.

"Jason, we have you in a slow climb in a left-hand spiral. Keep up the good work."

The atmosphere in Control relaxed a notch. It appeared to be only a matter of time before the submarine would breach, and Jason and Buddy would be recovered. The Captain had the bridge team put out the word to Pennypacker and the divers to be ready to conduct retrieval operations in one hour. Gordon nodded to Karen to follow him, and the two of them exited through the aft door.

She came to a stop in the hallway. "Professor, I don't want to get too far from the hologram."

"I don't either, but you and I never got to finish our conversation. What did you have to say to me?"

"I was hoping to get you to abort the dive before anything happened. Did you know there is a LAN still installed in this ship?"

"Yes. Duke mentioned it, but as far as I know, none of our ..."

"Professor, that network might be outdated but still active, and it could still access, well, everything. And that means no one would have to use a hammer to screw up our dives, just a laptop and a room with an outlet still in place. In fact I found one in my room."

Blake listened with growing comprehension and dismay to Karen's recitation. "For Pete's sake, all our other efforts to protect the submersibles, while all along there was an electronic Trojan Horse! What do you suggest we do?"

"Right now all I want is to see the sub on deck. I don't know what to tell you except that maybe there's a way to tell who's on the net and when they're using it."

"Good thinking. I'll ask Duke. Now let's get back inside and see how Jason and Buddy are doing."

Back inside, they got a report from Julian. "The Bird is now three thousand feet from the bottom. Jason is keeping the ascent at a low angle. It's rising very slowly, sir."

"Control, this is Jason. Passing six thousand-eight hundred feet."

"Roger. What is Buddy's condition?"

"He's awake but in pain. I have him lying between the passenger seats. I think he has a concussion."

Again Professor Blake reached for the mike. "Jason, Gordon here. It's possible that someone's been reprogramming the sub computers. We need you up as soon as possible."

Simson took the mike: "Can you give me a ballast light status?"

"No, and I don't know where to look."

"It's on the rear bulkhead behind you."

"Ah, I see them."

"Are all five rows lit up?"

"Um – yes. Affirmative."

Simson shut off the mike and turned to Gordon. "They're not out of the woods yet. Jason said he had released one bank of weights, but the lights go off when they fall free of the hull. Unless there's a signal error, the sub is still fully ballasted. That means they might not have enough engine power to reach the surface."

"What are we going to do about it?"

Karen had taken her post near the hologram with rising spirits until she heard this last exchange. Now she felt a rising panic and knew that if she stayed in the room she would make an emotional fool of herself. She needed to get some fresh air and get a grip.

The sunshine on the flight deck lifted her spirits and helped her focus on problem-solving, not self-pity or fear. She stood staring blankly at the vastness of the ocean that currently held someone she loved in its black deathly depths. It was an effort to push her mind into gear but she managed, assessing the facts as she knew them, looking blindly for a clue regarding who had tampered with the submarine's software. It could be anyone. But right now that person's identity was not as important as trying to figure out a way to access and reprogram the sub. She knew that once launched, Yellow Bird was on its own. But surely there must be some way for Jason to override erroneous commands. Jason had simply reversed the signals to the diving planes. What could he do to rectify other software glitches and release the ballast?

When Karen reentered the monitoring room, the Captain was still conferring with the others, and judging from the way he was shaking his head, they weren't coming up with any good ideas. The hologram showed disappointing progress as she marched right past it.

"Excuse me, Professor. I have an idea," she blurted out, her voice louder than she would have liked. "If Derek can give us the right answers."

Derek appeared at the edge of the group. "Fire away," he said.

"Okay. I saw you and Jason doing pre-flight checks on the sub the other day. You were using a laptop. Here's my question. Where do you stow it?"

"Well I keep it on the sub. I don't want anyone else using it."

"And how exactly do you send signals from your laptop to the sub's computer?"

"There's a computer jack on the bulkhead."

The Captain interrupted. "Just where is this taking us?"

Simson intervened. "Oh I get it. She's hoping that Derek checks the submarine's programs when down in the Bird by plugging directly into the submarine. If he can do that, then possibly so can Jason."

Derek brightened; his voice suddenly enthusiastic. "Well of course he can! Karen, you asked exactly the right question. If it's raining I sit in the sub to do my checks."

The Captain looked at Derek, then Simson and last at Karen. He actually smiled at her – maybe, just maybe, he had underestimated her.

"Jason, this is Simson. We have an idea. We want you to get out of your seat and move aft."

"I'm on my way."

"Good. So in the locker at the foot of the aft bulkhead you'll find a laptop. Bring it out."

There was a long period of silence. They wondered if they'd lost communication.

"Jason, did you copy?"

"I heard you! I'm trying to find the computer. I can't talk to you and look for it at the same time."

A full five minutes went by. Blake muttered under his breath, "Damn, he can't find it."

Derek murmured: "That's where I left it, unless someone else took it."

The Captain and Simson simply stared at the telephone speaker. Karen was speechless with anxiety.

"Hey, I found it!"

Jason's voice sounded triumphant. There were audible sighs from his listeners. Just the act of locating the laptop provided some semblance of progress, possibly even redemption.

"Jason, this is Derek. The laptop has a battery that lasts for several hours. Do not try to find an outlet for power. On the bulkhead to the right of the operator's seat you'll find a computer outlet. Do you see it?"

There was a long period of silence.

"I found it."

"Good. Fire up the laptop."

Derek quickly led him to a folder labeled Auxiliaries. "Now scroll down to Stability and click on it, then scroll down to the word Ballast. Click on it and look for a diagram."

Karen was getting impatient. She pulled at Derek's arm: "Isn't there a simpler way? What do you do for pre-flight checks?"

"I don't pre-flight the ballast system. That's a mechanical check done when the weights are stored and the bays are empty. We don't …"

"Derek, I have the diagram. It's very complicated."

"That's okay. We're going to edit the picture. Find a ballast hook in the diagram and click on it."

Jason was obviously not an engineer. It took what seemed like an eternity for him to respond. *"Okay, I have a ballast hook. And I see another list."*

"Yes, good. Now find the word Release and try clicking on it."

Nothing seemed to happen.

"Damn," someone muttered.

The hologram confirmed that the submarine was still pitched up but making no upward progress. Karen noted that the Bird had just crossed three thousand feet. The engine stopped. The Captain spoke to the operator, "Tell us if they start to sink."

Karen felt ready to burst into tears. She bit her lip and focused again on finding another approach to the rescue. As she stared at the meter showing depth of dive, she recalled that the sub had been at three thousand feet when the first problem had occurred. Was there something about that depth?

She approached Simson to tell him about her observation. "I'm just wondering, could someone use depth as an elicitor, a surrogate to issue commands to the rest of the system software?"

It took him a moment to focus on what she was saying. "I'd have to think about that. You may be onto something. Maybe Derek knows."

- 11 -
The Virus

~~~~~~~~~~~~~~~~

While the research team brainstormed ways to get the submarine to the surface, the two hostages waited in the black waters far below. The cabin was absolutely quiet except for Buddy's breathing, which was shallow but rhythmic. An ongoing flow of sea creatures which Jason could see out the ports seemed to be mocking him. "Invader. Alien. You don't belong down here." And then something crossed his field of view, high and to the left, like a dark cloud on an otherwise clear night. But it was gone before he got a good look at it.

At this point he knew his survival hung on the efforts they were making topside to affect a rescue. His sanity felt like it hung on their reassurances that it was only a matter of time before they'd solve the dilemma. But time ticking away by the second was his enemy, testing his patience and toying with his imagination. Time by the hour was his friend, assuring him that there was plenty of it left. But was there?

The oxygen supply when fully charged was designed to keep four passengers alive for about five days. He checked the gauges and assured himself that there was enough for the two of them for a week. But all that air would be a slow-motion death curse if the Bird sank again to the ocean floor where the two of them would await the inevitable ... beyond help and beyond hope.

Jason looked at the depth sensor. His breathing tensed another notch. They were very slowly sinking. He could almost feel the massive pressure outside the sub, pushing in at him with almost murderous intent. And really – who was it up on the ship who was so very cleverly committing this deadly crime?

Karen found Derek on the mess deck getting a cup of coffee before returning to the monitoring room. She asked: "Will you listen to another theory about the computer program?"

They sat down together. She could see the extreme tension in his face, but he nodded for her to begin. "So then, Jason and Buddy had just reported crossing three thousand feet when they lost control of the sub."

"Yes, I recall now."

"And then when they were ascending, they were again crossing three thousand feet when the propulsion system stopped. I think there might be a software command, a virus really, that started overriding the submarine's programs at that depth."

"Hmm. So you think that whoever the hacker is, he wants to make absolutely sure that if he doesn't do them in on the way down, they aren't going to make it back up."

"Exactly. Simson is up in the monitoring room looking over the tech manuals. Can you help him?" The words had tumbled out in a rush, betraying her anxiety. Derek, however, was impressed with her perception. The depth trigger made a lot of sense.

They returned to the monitoring room where a glance at the hologram showed the Bird suspended where they had last observed it. Simson was engrossed in his research, and the others stood around the telephone table, looking lost. Derek approached Simson.

"Have you found anything?"

"No. I think Karen is right on the money, but I can't see where the erroneous command would have been introduced. Nothing depends on depth to determine its operation. Well, except for the bladder."

"Well isn't it possible that the signal could get tapped in somewhere along the way?"

"I don't see how but I'll take another look."

The speaker from the sub came suddenly alive with Jason's urgent voice. *"Alert! We are descending!"*

Everyone within earshot fixed their attention on the hologram. The operator readjusted the scale. The sub was again down below three thousand feet, sinking slowly but perceptibly.

"Jason, we hear you. Is the bladder heated to one hundred and sixty degrees?"

"The bladder reached temperature as we ascended through three thousand feet."

"Well it should slow your descent and stabilize at four thousand feet. In the meantime we're working on your computer problem."

"Hey, I can't just sit here! How about maybe you get smart and find the source of all this. Find him! He's the one who knows how to bring the Bird topside."

"Yes, well, we'll definitely see what we can do."

"You do that. It's just slightly scary down here."

His mike went dead.

Simson had been working his way through the tech manuals, bouncing ideas off Derek and the others without any positive result. Karen was doubly frustrated. She wanted more than life itself to find a way to rescue Jason, but she was totally unequipped to interpret blueprints or provide any tech advice.

Her mind wandered and she found herself considering the probable consequences this massive failure would generate for the company providing the ship and sub. Still wounded by their encounter earlier in the day, she took a thoughtless jab at Captain Pearson, "I wonder what your boss is going to think when he sees the replay of what we did with his submarine?"

The Captain offered no reaction, treating her as if she didn't even exist. But Simson turned on her. "What did you just say?"

"I said something about what Frontier Explorers is going to think when they replay and evaluate the dive. I'm sorry, I shouldn't have said anything."

Simson's reaction scared her. He grabbed her by her shoulders and literally shook her. "My God, Karen, that's it – the black box. All pertinent information gets recorded there. That's the one link between the depth readings and the controls. They all feed it. Come on, Derek, let's start all over. Captain, we'll have an answer in fifteen minutes. I'll get the blueprints out of my safe."

"Jason, this is Simson. We have another program for you to try, but first you have to do some rewiring for us."

Jason's crackly voice spoke up. *"Hey, I'd do open heart surgery on myself if I thought it would help."*

Simson explained where the flight recorder was located and how to disconnect it. It turned out that isolating the box was a simple three-step procedure which Jason was fully capable of doing.

"Simson, I have disconnected the junction box and reconnected the wires."

"Good. Now try to restart the engine."

Simson muted the mike and turned to Professor Blake. "If the propellers turn he should have sufficient propulsion to start for the surface, but he won't have the buoyancy to get all the way up, and we don't know what the controls might do as he passes three thousand feet."

"Simson, I have propulsion! We are moving!"

"Do not attempt to apply too much power. You are moving away from us."

"Do you want me to try the controls?"

"Yes. Try them."

Jason decided to try a turn before he tampered with depth. He applied some pressure to the left. The gyrocompass barely moved. Losing his patience, he applied power and pressed the stick harder. The compass started to spin slowly and then faster.

"Simson, I have steering control. I am going to attempt to climb."

Now that he had control of the submarine, Jason moved his hand to the ballast switches and repeated the commands he had entered when he and Lipscomb were just over the ocean floor. He jettisoned one bank and turned to examine the indicator lights to observe the results.

There was no change in status. His heart froze. In spite of his ability to steer and propel the submarine, he had no control over the weights.

"Simson, I cannot dump ballast."

"Roger." A new voice. Derek was now on the phone. "Get your laptop and scroll to the print that has the ballast hooks on it."

They walked Jason through the preliminary steps to search for 'Release.' "Do not try 'Open,' we think that is a circuit command. I repeat, do not click on 'Open.' Click on 'Release.'"

"Control, I am pressing 'Release' now."

Jason turned his head to watch the ballast lights. He clicked the mouse and a whole row of lights went out. It wasn't what he'd expected – he assumed that the ballast hook illustration represented only one weight – it now seemed every weight in the row had been jettisoned. The realization had his spirits soaring. He and Buddy were on their way to the surface.

"Derek, one whole row of indicator lights has gone out!"

Karen started to cheer, but the Captain waved for her to be quiet. The others took their cue from him. Lights are just lights. Everyone turned to look at the hologram.

"Roger, Jason. We are watching your progress."

"Control, we are approaching three thousand feet."

Karen had an idea. She made her way over to touch Derek's forearm. "Don't you think we should have Jason cross the threshold in as neutral a posture as possible? Slow and level?"

"Good idea." With a nod of agreement from Captain Pearson, who was listening to the conversation, Derek called the sub: "Jason, level off and slow to bare steerageway. Do not attempt to release any more weights. Minimize control signals."

Jason understood. They would be crossing the minefield again very soon.

Jason centered the stick and reduced power, glancing at the gauges and staring out the port. He had no doubt that they were in a state of positive buoyancy. Not trusting the accuracy of the depth sensor nor the apparent depth sounder, he decided to let the sub rise through at least two hundred more feet before testing the controls and proceeding with the ascent.

"Control, we are rising slowly toward three thousand. Over."

There was no response. Jason attempted to reach them again. Still no reply. He knew these dives were subject to communications blackouts, so the situation didn't unsettle him. Besides, the gauges confirmed what he was hoping for. The submersible slowly approached and rose above three thousand feet. He was elated.

But he knew that Buddy was in serious trouble. He climbed out of his seat and reached for the first-aid kit, found some iodine and cotton swabs, and attempted to dress the big cut in Buddy's forehead. The application must have been painful because he flinched and opened his eyes.

"Jason, what are you doing?"

Jason explained their situation as clearly as he could, and offered the injured man aspirin and a sip of their limited supply of water. Then he returned to his seat and took another round of readings, deciding to wait another one hundred feet or ten minutes, whichever came first, and then try out the controls.

He looked out the porthole but there was nothing to see. But hold on, there should be plenty to see. Why was the port dark? Jason recalled the momentary dark cloud he had seen when descending and what'd happened on the test dive – that entirely-unexplained encounter with a seemingly huge curtain of darkness accompanied by the communications failure and loss of the hologram.

"Control, can you hear me? Control?"

There was no response. He decided impulsively to give the submarine full power and attempt a steep climb, jettisoning weight as they ascended.

"What's going on?"

It was Buddy, whose voice was stronger than Jason expected. Jason turned in his seat. "I don't know. I can't raise the ship, and I can't see anything out of the port. I'm going to try to get us out of here."

Jason pushed the throttle to maximum and pulled on the stick. The sub responded, lifting its nose. He then turned his attention to the laptop and located the illustration for the ballast hook. Why was there only one displayed on the print, the same one he'd already clicked on. Where were the others?

Suddenly the sub weas jolted hard by a collision with something out there. The impact slid the computer off Jason's knees onto the deck at his feet. He found himself lifting his arms to protect his face, but the sub was only moving at around four knots through the water. Jason peered out into the darkness through his port. Whatever was out there had not shown itself nor responded in any perceptible way, and mercifully the sub hadn't pitched up or rolled over.

Easing back on the throttle, Jason released the stick. There was no point in repeatedly ramming whatever they had hit. One thing he knew beyond a doubt was that he wasn't going to try to evade by putting the sub into a dive. What he needed was more information. He weighed turning on the spotlights but instead decided to turn off the cabin lights and instrument panels. If this creature-thing went dark to hide, then the sub would, too.

He looked out of the port again and imagined all sorts of strange monsters out there haunting the sub. He saw nothing. It was a standoff. Nothing to see. Everything to fear. Time painfully invisibly went by as the sub continued its slow decelerating ascent. Jason couldn't see the gauges, and he couldn't sense any change in depth. Unwilling to turn back on any lights, he couldn't do anything with the laptop or manipulate the controls. Buddy moaned in pain and likely in terror.

For all Jason knew, they were suspended in the depths waiting for nothing and preparing to die. The darkness and the cramped space consumed him. What was out there! What did it plan to do to him next? His only hope was to reach the surface. To do nothing was to know nothing. So Jason shifted again into action, switching on the instrument panels first.

A quick glance greeted him with good news: they had ascended another two hundred feet. He then looked out of the porthole to see if there was any reaction or change. Darkness still enveloped them. He turned on the cabin lights and reached for the laptop, hastily reaching the illustrated ballast hook. His fingers were shaking. He felt that at any second he would be interrupted again, thwarting his efforts to lighten the submersible. Instinct told him that one bank of weights was not enough to return them to the surface.

Suddenly the porthole next to him was bathed by a shimmering glow. What was that? Almost panicking, he worked even faster, fearing that his own emotions would disable his efforts to reach the drawing and issue the appropriate software commands. Wasting no time to get a better look at whatever was there, he concentrated all his energy on jettisoning ballast.

Something passed so close that it nudged the sub and rolled it to port about fifteen degrees. Unnerved by the jolt, Jason clutched the computer and braced his feet against the instrument panel. Buddy moaned in pain, and some equipment that had come loose shifted again. He heard them bump up against the bulkhead.

Then – nothing more. Jason now had the blueprint on the screen. He moved the mouse to the sidebar menu and searched for 'Commands.' But just then he felt the stern lift, as if there were a following sea. The nose pitched down, and he feared they were going to roll over the way Buddy and Derek had. He wrapped his arms around the laptop, as if protecting a football from an aggressive tackle. If anything happened to the computer, they would perish.

The submarine pitched down about forty-five degrees and then started to lift fast. Buddy shrieked as he slid forward feet first into the instrument panel. All the debris that had rolled to port now slid forward, collecting under the forward seat. Jason was thrown against the stick, gouging his arms and stomach as he lifted the computer clear of the controls.

Then he felt the stern start to settle. He glanced and saw that the gauges showed that the sub was rising even faster now. The curtain of sparkling lights that had recently been dancing in the water to starboard now appeared to port. Whatever was out there was circling them, toying with them, perhaps setting up for an attack. Jason fleetingly hoped against hope that the creature might be attempting to buoy them upward.

Jason had been just one click away from redeeming them, but as he opened the cover again, expecting to see the sidebar menu, he gaped at a message saying he'd shut down the computer improperly. Resisting a string of curses, he rebooted the laptop. He could feel another movement as the sub rolled to starboard slightly and then rolled back. He was breathing heavily as he clicked on the ballast hook, still wondering why only one image appeared. The cursor reached the button marked 'Release' and Jason clicked.

The submarine started to roll to starboard again. Jason repeated the command to release more weights. Each time he did so, another row of lights extinguished themselves. He continued the process until all the lights were out and all the steel weights jettisoned. He felt convinced that no matter what happened to the controls, if Whateveritwas didn't damage the sub, they would continue to ascend to daylight.

Movement outside the porthole now occupied all of Jason's attention. The light had disappeared from his side of the submarine, and now he could see a glow to port. What was going on? Buddy lay in the aisle between the seats – nothing more Jason could do for him right now. He switched off the cabin lights and the instrument panel again. The creature hadn't made any further moves on the sub.

The lights outside blinked out. Once again the sub was immersed in total darkness. Jason reflected on what had just taken place and decided to attempt a little experiment. Each time he had extinguished the cabin lights, the creature had vanished. When he turned them back on, the glow reappeared in the cabin ports. In an effort to see if the creature would respond, Jason turned on every light available to him, including the spotlights.

He was rewarded with an immediate brilliant display of shimmering light that virtually encompassed the boat. Weighted with exhaustion and overwhelmed by relief, Jason burst into a laugh. Imprisoned in this submarine, his giddiness seemed perverse; but no matter, they were on their way to the surface! He slapped at the switches, shutting off the spotlights and overhead illumination along with the instrument panel. Peering through the starboard porthole, he grinned as the galaxy of sparkles suddenly and once again disappeared.

He switched on the lights. *"Control, this is Jason. Do you hear me? Do you hear me? Over."* But the telephone remained mute. The inability to reach *Aladdin* was demoralizing. Would the ship even be there when they surfaced?

Then by its illumination the creature revealed itself again to him. The water surrounding the sub was aglow, and Jason saw a vast sheet of light cross ahead of the sub from the left, seeming to fold itself and dive under the cabin, as if providing a blanket under the rising hull. Jason caught just a glimpse of what appeared to be large plate-like eyes and a long scoop of a mouth as the creature doubled back under him. He waited for several breathless moments for the gigantic fish, eel, octopus or whatever to complete its maneuver. When there was no more light to starboard, Jason pressed the throttle full ahead, pulled back on the stick and banked to the right. The submarine responded to his signals and climbed into a twenty-five-degree angle of pitch, accelerating the rate of climb as they rose above eighteen hundred feet on their way to the surface.

Jason kept his eyes fixed on the gauges and the compass, purposely not looking out of the port for fear he would be intimidated into some other maneuver. When the compass showed that he had turned a full ninety degrees from the creature, he straightened out with only one intent – to outstrip the thing by reaching water it perhaps couldn't survive in.

As they passed fourteen hundred feet, Jason began to relax. Given the depth at which the fish had first appeared, surely they were out of reach now. He turned to check on Buddy, to see if he was at least conscious, when the light Jason recognized appeared in the port over his recumbent passenger. The creature easily overtook the submarine, snaked over the top, and wound down to starboard. It made no apparent attempt to touch the hull but continued its gyrations as they climbed.

Aboard *Aladdin* Gordon shook his head. "OKAY," he uttered with a sigh. "It has been over an hour. I'll call the office. We need help. We need to let them know what has happened."

But Captain Pearson was not ready to do so. "Hold on. We don't yet know what really happened. We have nothing that we can tell them yet. We need to wait for a signal. Then we'll know."

Gordon looked past the Captain at Aaron and said to all those present. "I think we should have let someone know already."

Pearson bristled. "What good would it do? If the sub is lost, do you think there is anything, anything in the world that we can get out here in time to rescue them? Either they are fine, or they ..."

"*Control, this is Jason. Do you hear me? Over.*"

The debate was forgotten in a mad scramble to join Simson who had reached the telephone first. "Jason. Jason. We hear you! Thank God. Over."

"*We are approaching the ...*"

"We have the submarine on the hologram!"

Blake waved his hand in irritation at the operator. *"... and we need immediate assistance."*

The hologram showed that they would surface shortly, and at their rate of ascent their return would be spectacular. And ... indeed, the Bird literally flew up out of the water under full throttle. It was some distance from the ship, but those on deck got the show of their lives, suddenly witnessing with no warning this great yellow metallic whale breaching for all it was worth.

- 12 -
Evening

~~~~~~~~~~~~~~~~

By the time the conning officer had maneuvered *Aladdin* to a position alongside the bobbing submarine, Karen had reclaimed her vantage point on the flight deck while the others assembled on the fantail. The Captain had responsibilities there; the others simply wanted a closer look. Working in twilight, the divers connected the halyard efficiently in spite of the worsening weather.

The halyard was winched in, dragging the submersible to a position directly under the A-frame. The Bird emerged from the water dripping triumphantly as it arched over the transom. As the submarine reached its apex the hatch popped open and Jason's head emerged. From his perch high over the deck, the yellow hull obscured most of the crew below, but directly in front of him stood Karen Finch, staring back at him in wide-eyed relief.

Buddy and Jason were taken to sick bay for medical attention. Jason's blood pressure and heart rate were elevated but otherwise he was fit. Buddy on the other hand was in serious condition. Jason had correctly diagnosed his companion's broken rib, but the more serious injury was his head wound. The blood in his eye had come from a minor cut, but at some point he had also suffered a concussion. He was put under observation, and the decision was made to proceed east to rendezvous with a helicopter for a medical evacuation.

"The MEDEVAC dictates our next course of action, doesn't it, Gordon?" Aaron asked. "It's obviously time to head for shore. Saboteur or no saboteur, we're finished out here. We can't take that sub down again. When Frontier Explorers hears what happened they'll withdraw their permission for any more dives."

Gordon responded with resignation. "Yeah, we'll meet the helo, transfer Buddy, and then head for San Diego. The weather's expected to deteriorate anyway. But we're not done here. We've paid for twelve weeks so we have almost four weeks left on the contract. Duke gets to refuel a week earlier than planned, that's all."

"Fair enough." Aaron said. "But what about the possibility that nothing has been an accident? How do you explain what happened today?"

Blake looked too tired to deal with the question. "Right now, I don't know."

Karen was waiting for him in the passageway outside sick bay, leaning up against the bulkhead. Jason's sudden appearance at the door startled her. She straightened up and simply stared at him awkwardly. He stood in the door regarding her, uncertain what to do. Then they both closed the gap between them, and with a mutual audible sigh of relief wrapped their arms around each other. The kiss that would have followed the hug was stolen from them by the noisy approach of footsteps. They pushed back. It was only a member of the crew, but the moment was lost.

The cook kept the galley open late for all hands. Gordon, Aaron and Karen joined Jason for dinner. After the long day in the sub he was famished and exhausted, but after the hot meal and black coffee he was also outraged that somewhere among the passengers and crew there lurked a man who had tried to kill him.

"It all seemed so theoretical until Buddy and I were trapped down there," he muttered. "Then it hit me hard that someone on board had done this to us, and I tell you," he grumbled in anger to his three dinner companions, "whoever it is should hope and pray that I'm not the one who gets to him first."

The others looked at him without sharing their thoughts. Gordon felt ashamed that he had pressed to launch the submersible today and that he'd thought himself so clever with his little stratagem to put Buddy aboard. He didn't know where to go from here. To do nothing was not an option. They had to root out whoever was responsible for the string of mishaps. They would likely need the police, but that would mean the end of the project.

Jason continued, "Gordon, you do realize that by returning to San Diego, you're giving the murderer a chance to get away. He's trapped right now. Can we at least delay our return or slow the ship to buy a little time?"

Aaron interrupted whatever response the Professor was preparing to make. "'Murderer' is a little strong, isn't it? After all, you and Buddy are safe aboard."

It was the wrong thing to say. Jason flared. "You still don't get it, do you! We're alive because of one hell of a lot of effort and good luck. Do you by any possible stretch of your imagination think that we were supposed to get back? Is this guy any less a murderer because his plan failed? If you had been down there you wouldn't be so smug!"

Aaron flushed with anger and embarrassment. "Jason, I'm going to write your disrespect off to stress. This has been a long day for all of us. I think you ought to get some sleep. We can discuss what to do next in the morning." He grabbed his napkin off his lap and threw it on the table. "Gordon, I'm going to my stateroom. Perhaps you and I can talk later."

He slid his chair back and left. They watched him go. "I'm sorry about that, Gordon," Jason growled without remorse, "but this is deadly serious and we've got to do something."

The Professor looked at him without smiling. "Yes, it's serious and we'll act, but you have got a lot to learn. Don't alienate Aaron. If we're going to find this guy we'll need teamwork. We've all been under a great deal of stress today. Let's get some sleep and meet early in the morning, say seven sharp?"

The Professor excused himself, leaving Karen alone with Jason. She reached out her hand and put it gently over his. "I do think you need some sleep," she said gently. "Let me walk you to your stateroom. Tomorrow, we'll dig in and catch whoever's doing this to us."

They left the mess deck in silence. When they got to his door, he asked her to come in. "I just need to talk a little before going to sleep," he said. "I have urged Gordon to stay at sea in spite of all that's happening. Two reasons. I still think we can get the job done, and if the ship returns to port, the replacements will show up. This guy will walk, rotated right out."

He unlocked his door, and they entered his compartment. He locked the door behind them, offered her his chair and sat heavily on the bunk, looking at her with exhausted bloodshot eyes.

"What happened on shore before, that was different from trying to murder somebody," he said to her. "I think we're maybe facing a conspiracy. If we can nab one of them we may find out who's behind all this."

Karen hesitated. She was dead tired too but still emotionally charged. "Well, thank God you're still alive," she said softly, her voice vulnerable. "I thought I'd die several times when it seemed you were lost."

She got tears in her eyes and stopped talking, choking up. Jason slipped off his shoes. "I thought of you a hundred times down there," he said, his voice also softening with emotion. "I'm still blown away from the experience. There was something down there, Karen.

Something messing with the sub but not damaging it – almost helping in fact. But I have no idea what."

"Horrible," she muttered.

"But I have absolutely no concrete data to offer, no idea what it was or what it was doing. The only thing I am certain of is that somebody on board this ship is using deadly and also quite ingenious tactics to keep us from completing this research."

They sat in silence for a moment, staring into each other's eyes.

"Well, you and I," she told him with deep conviction, "we're going to find out who."

"Yes. It's going to take a lot of work and there isn't much time."

Jason frowned with a new thought. "Gordon said he was going to call the office in the morning. Do you know of anything he might have found out?"

"No. And Jason, you look ready to pass out any moment. What matters right now is that you survived. We can talk about all this in the morning."

She came over to him, bent down and kissed him gently on the lips, then turned and left him.

After Gordon left the mess deck he headed for Aaron's stateroom to smooth things over. He couldn't afford to have his closest ally alienated by one of his proteges. He admired the Chief Scientist and depended on his advice. They had known each other for a long, long time. Jason was an exceptional scholar, who would someday have a national reputation. It would be a shame if today's acrimony damaged his promising career.

Aaron was waiting for him. His door was open and he was standing in the middle of his stateroom. "Thanks for coming by, Gordon. I don't think I'll be able to work with your young man again."

The tone was off-putting, the announcement some sort of formal declaration. Gordon was amused at the pout that accompanied his friend's announcement. They would get by this.

He closed the door behind him. "I am very sorry for what took place this evening, but I think you should forgive Jason for his outburst. I can't even imagine going through what he went through today. He's a hero in my book, and probably his safe return has kept you and I from prosecution."

The last remark jolted Aaron. "Prosecution? You're serious, aren't you."

"You and I need to have a conference call in the morning with our sponsors and the leadership at Frontier Explorers, but our real problem is what to do about the criminal activity we've experienced out here. Jason can be a big help, and he's also one of the few people I trust. Will you please help me? Work with us?"

"Well, haven't I always?"

"I know it's been difficult with you busy working for mining companies, and I motivated by my concerns about the environment."

"It's not that," Aaron said. "We're both scientists looking for the deeper truth and right action. But now we're suddenly caught up in attempted murder. Unbelievable!"

"Attempted murder at least. And we probably have too little time to solve it unless we can keep the ship at sea for longer than just two days. We're still scheduled for at least two more weeks out here. And we can still run your sled experiments."

"But what if the saboteur tries to do something drastic again to block that?" Aaron asked. "I do think we must call in the authorities. We need a full investigation, and that means getting outside help."

"No. Not if we can help it. That would instantly halt our research."

"Gordon, we're dealing with a murderer here!"

"If your mining companies get a greenlight they'll probably cause deadly world-wide damage."

"No, I keep telling you, Gordon, we can trust them to make the right environmental decisions."

"But only if we get data to guide them!"

"Ah, yes. You're right."

"We can do this ourselves. We can check the LAN message exchanges like Karen has suggested. Had someone in fact been tampering with the software? And can those commands be traced to their source?"

"We'll need to bring the Communications man in on this," Kline said. "Is he trustworthy?"

"He's not on any of our lists. I say yes, he's okay. And we'll need him for some of the tech work."

"Good – so that's a start … for tomorrow. Listen, I'm ready to drop. Let's call it a night."

As Gordon opened the door to head back to his stateroom, he heard footsteps and saw the back of someone hurrying away down the passageway and around a corner out of sight. Turning around, he spoke urgently to Kline, "I think someone was outside our door listening!"

"Probably just a crewmember passing by," Kline responded. "Leave it alone and get some sleep."

Karen walked to her stateroom feeling increasing worry and anger over the events of the day. The project was a bust as far as she was concerned. All the enthusiastic conversations she had with the Professor and Jason kept replaying in her mind. It had all been so futile, and almost ended in utter tragedy.

She could feel the sand in her eyes, knew that she was bone-weary. But she couldn't bring herself to put aside any longer the question that had plagued her all day. What might they learn from the LAN? Hale in Communications would be the one to turn to, but he would be asleep by now. If she were to call him, he would probably just get angry.

She reached her door and started to unlock and turn the handle. Then she had an idea, an urge to go see if there was someone on watch in Communications this time of night, someone who was not aware at all of the conspiracy theory, who might very well give her some off-hand information of value. Turning back down the passageway, she reached the stairs and hurried up to the Communications room, located directly under the bridge.

The door was closed but there was a light on inside. She knocked softly. A long moment later the door opened partway.

"What can I do for you?" The man who confronted her looked suspiciously at Karen. His position and stance clearly indicated that she was not going a step further. She had expected a warmer reception, if only because of the loneliness she assumed everyone felt on watch late at night. It appeared instead that she was intruding.

"Hi, I'm Karen Finch, a summer intern." She smiled as brightly as she could at midnight after a terribly long day. "I couldn't sleep. I've seen most of the ship but not the Communications room. I know it's late but could you maybe give me a quick tour?"

The man looked perplexed. "Oh, well what do you want to see? We've got radios and computers and piles of paper, plus a telephone and the satellite links. Come on in."

He backed away from the door, which he now fully opened so that she could see the extent of the small space. "There's not much else in here. Well there's the ship's computer network of course."

"Oh, you've got a lot of equipment packed in here! But it must be a drag to work the night shift."

The operator smiled ruefully. "Mr. Hale, he keeps me always on the night watches, he covers the ship's communications during the day when most of the inflow happens, says there is some sensitive stuff for the Captain that I'm not cleared for."

"Are you also responsible for the computers on the ship, and what's it called – the Local Area Network? I hear that takes a lot of work keeping it up."

"That's not my department," he said defensively. "We just operate the equipment; we don't fix it." He returned to more-familiar ground. "Did I tell you about our backup emergency communications that we can use if the satellite link fails?"

Karen ignored him. "If you don't maintain the computers and the network, then who does?"

"I don't know but the Ship's Secretary could probably tell you."

Karen felt it was time to go. "I see. Well you were very kind to give me so much of your time. Thank you. May I come back?"

"Any time."

She attempted another engaging smile, felt it wilt, and left him standing in the passageway watching her depart. Tomorrow, or was it today? She would find the man who could tell her what she needed to know.

- 13 -
Lights Off

~~~~~~~~~~~~~~~~

In spite of getting about six hours of sleep, Karen woke up with a jolt and wasted no time getting herself ready for the day. She knew that Gordon would huddle with Aaron and the Captain to make plans, and she guessed that Jason would be included too. In an effort to see him before the others monopolized him, she padded down the passageway to knock softly on his door.

There was no answer. Darn. She was on her own. As she headed for breakfast she noted that the weather had begun to deteriorate. *Aladdin* was beginning to pitch in the long rolling seas. After an ample meal, she located the Secretary, who affirmed that he was indeed responsible for the ship's computer network but that a man named Bert Hamblin was the hands-on systems administrator.

Hamblin's office was a cubicle just outside the main engineering spaces. He was a cheerful pudgy man in his forties who greeted Karen enthusiastically and asked without hesitation: "What is it in particular that you want to know?"

"Oh, nothing important. Yesterday I noticed that I had a computer jack in my stateroom. Do all the staterooms have them? If so, I'm going to suggest that Professor Blake and his team use them."

He nodded. "The entire ship was wired quite a while back. The network covers all the staterooms on the Main Deck, the deck below, and every space in the superstructure above the Main Deck. Oh, and we have outlets here, of course, and in two or three locations in Engineering. We keep it operational in case the ship Wi-Fi goes out. The crew can write to each other, access a central database, and operate some remote equipment on the bridge and in engineering."

Karen's adrenaline was suddenly beginning to pump. "Wow, that's quite complex. Can you monitor the communications, too?"

He hesitated before he spoke. "I'm not sure what you mean by 'monitor.' I don't spy on people if that's what you mean!"

"No. No. I was just wondering if the ship keeps a database of the transmissions on the net. Can you tell who is using the network and when?"

Bert's suspicions had been piqued. "Possibly, some of that. Why do you ask?"

"Oh, it's just because Professor Blake is a bit touchy about confidentiality with his research data, you know."

"Well get me some time with the Professor and I'll make your case. Get him all set up in his stateroom using his laptop. Nobody much uses it these days like I said, so there's no worry about eavesdroppers."

At around ten in the morning, Jason woke up slowly and unwillingly. He had a slight headache and a dry mouth. It felt like a hangover until jolting memories of the previous day rolled in on him. He recalled the claustrophobia he'd felt in the sub. The darkness of his stateroom felt intolerably confining. He urgently needed fresh air and more space.

There were an unusual number of people on the mess deck when he got there, and no one looked very happy. Jason wrote the mood off to worsening weather until Julian Phelps accosted him. "I guess you've heard about the change in our schedule."

"No, I haven't heard, I just woke up."

"Well, we're heading northeast to meet the helo. Once the helo picks up Buddy later today, we're going to stay on track for San Diego to get help."

The news stunned Jason. He had been overruled without a chance to appeal. Blake had given up.

The helicopter landing conditions were a repeat of the ones Karen and the Professor had experienced a week before. Dealing with the worsening sea, the helicopter flew in over the starboard quarter but flared when it appeared the deck was rising too quickly under it. As they made their second approach, the deck fell away as the airframe was positioned over the ship. The pilot was signaled to hold his position until the stern started to rise. At just the right moment he was given the signal to land. After one bounce he set the helo firmly on deck, and it was tied down.

Buddy appeared on a stretcher carried by two members of the crew, escorted by the ship's doctor. The passenger door slid open, and one of the helicopter crewmembers assisted in loading him aboard. In less than ten minutes the entire procedure was complete and the helicopter was a fading image in the gray sky. The weather was expected to get a lot worse. With Buddy safely on his way to a mainland hospital, the ship settled down for the trip shoreward.

Before the final decision had been made to proceed to San Diego, key telephone calls had been placed and e-mail messages sent. They would be pier side in two days. While the medical evacuation had occupied the crew, Jason had gone looking for Gordon and Aaron. He found them in the Professor's stateroom. They both smiled at him. "Did you sleep well? You needed it." Aaron said in at least a somewhat friendly voice, a peace offering.

"The rumor on the mess deck," Jason said bluntly, "is that we are heading in."

"It's no rumor," Gordon admitted. "We're going back. You made a compelling argument about our dangerous predicament last night at dinner – before your face fell into your soup." He did not laugh. "We definitely need to sort things out, but we aren't equipped to deal with it. We need help."

"But ..."

"Hold on." Gordon stopped him. "Yesterday a message from the office came in on the employee files. The fact is, we're not getting consistent information. Also, Karen came by this morning to say she paid a visit to the Communications room last night after we went to bed."

"Oh?"

"They're not responsible for maintaining the Local Area Network, so this morning she went to the Ship's Secretary who introduced her to a fellow named Bert Hamblin, the Systems Administrator, the SYSAD for the ship's network. It seems he can isolate individual messages and their source. She's in her stateroom playing with the net right now to see what she can find out without alerting the saboteur."

"Well I'll go find out how she's doing."

Jason knocked quietly on her door. When he didn't hear a response, he just stood silently outside her stateroom, trying to work out how he was really feeling toward her. Something had changed while he was down deep. He was remembering how he'd felt that she was with him in the sub.

Desperately wanting to see her, he called out, "Karen, it's me." At first, there was no response from inside her room, but then suddenly the door opened wide and there she was.

They just looked at each other for a moment, not smiling, not speaking, just taking each other in. Then they both exhaled at the same time and came into each other's arms and held tight for an almost painfully gripping hug. Finally they let go and stepped back slightly, but still close. They were holding hands.

"Jason," she whispered. "I had to hold you tight to be sure you're really still here in the flesh."

"I'm regrouping," he smiled. "I play tough, but I'm not really. I was scared to death down there. You were with me all the way, I felt it."

And they came into each other's arms again and into their first real kiss, which had a hungry heat to it.

Then it was over. They were pushing back catching their breaths as they glanced bashfully into each other's eyes. "I wanted so badly to do that last night," she confessed.

Karen's mood dramatically shifted. "Jason, someone on this ship tried to kill you. We've got to find him before, well before he actually does kill somebody."

"Hopefully," Jason said, "now that the research is scuttled he'll back off."

"Scuttled? What do you mean 'scuttled'?"

"We're on our way to San Diego."

"I woke up shivering with the fear that there's some seriously insane creep on board that we see every day, some very brilliant lunatic who's playing games with our lives. I find myself studying the expression of everyone I encounter on board, searching for something that'll give him away. Oh, Jason, what are we going to do? Tell me, who do you suspect? Please, come sit down, talk to me."

He sat down on her bed, and without thinking smoothed out her blanket and pillow a bit, then raised his head and looked intently right at her. "Okay," he said, "let's be pragmatic. No one should be off the list. First, there's me and Buddy. Obviously we're not the bad guys. We've already eliminated the Captain. And there's you – well, I'd bet my life, again, that you're entirely in the clear." He smiled at the thought. "But we have to consider the professor and Dr. Kline, even them. Do they have any motive at all?"

She just sat there on her chair for a moment staring into space. "Gordon would be impossible."

"Even if a mining company slipped him a clean million into an offshore account?"

"Even then he wouldn't sabotage what he believes in. I feel I know him that well. But Aaron is another matter altogether."

"No, I … Well, yeah. He's a big question mark for me too. We can't say anything to Gordon though."

"And I'm not ready to discount the Captain. He's a hateful man."

"But he'd lose everything he's worked so hard for. He loves being captain of a ship. It's his whole life."

Jason moved on. "Down below, I had the feeling that full-out murder wasn't necessarily intended, but I don't know. If somebody was controlling the computers, they could make anything happen."

He fell silent a moment, again staring off into space. "Karen, there's something else."

"What?"

"Tampering with computers wasn't the only thing affecting our dive. There was something down there, like before. No question. Something alive and very big and also playing with the sub, but maybe actually helping. I have a debriefing in an hour. I guess I need to tell them."

Jason shook his head, visibly dismissing the memory. "Back to our list. There's Derek who knows everything about the sub. He's got to be on our list. As the stand-in operator, he could be doing it."

"I don't get those vibes at all from him, but we keep him on the list. Again, that million bucks …"

"And there's Simson Turner," Jason went on. "He designed the sub. I can't believe he'd sabotage his own creation, but then again …"

Karen was making notes at her small desk. "Yeah, that's a stretch. But who else? Let's get them all on the table, just between the two of us."

"There's Jonas Pennypacker, he'd have access," Jason went on. "And also anyone on his equipment crew. And there's Billy McCullough and the others in Control, and Charlie Hale in Communications plus at least half a dozen others."

"It's no good," Karen admitted, "there's even more, considering everybody working in the lab and the guys on the Captain's crew. Our list is simply too long. We can't possibly pare it down in just two days. Jason, the fact is, someone attempted to kill you and Buddy. We need the Captain to make a call to fly professionals, police detectives, here to take over."

"Hold on, let's stay calm, stay logical. The person doing all this must have previous knowledge of the electronics and computers that run the sub. That narrows our list, right? Who else can we discard?"

"Well what if there's two, not just one?" she asked tersely. "What if ..."

"Karen, stop. I'm feeling totally confused. Here's what I know. I don't want to see a single passenger leave this ship before I know in my heart that he isn't the man who tried to kill me. And for now, we can perhaps logically eliminate a few suspects before the police take over. I'm not ready to quit. You work on the LAN. I'm going to go back over our files and the roster of everyone on board. What we need is a clear motive."

"Jason, hold on. If we find him what are we going to do?"

"Let's take this one step at a time. Are we agreed we don't talk to anyone else about our list, not even Gordon?"

"I think that's being a bit extreme," she countered. "Don't we need to work with at least Gordon and the Captain?"

"For now, let's stay mum. We'll know when it's time to talk to them. Let's get to work, then have lunch together. I'll be in my stateroom."

He paused just a moment as he left to blow her a quick kiss from the door.

Aaron was overseeing some work in the lab when a messenger entered and handed him an envelope from Communications. The envelope contained a message from the home office concerning Harold Litton, one of the lab technicians now working on a project at the next table. The typed message was to alert him to Litton's previous employment with a competitor, Deep Ocean Research.

Stapled to the message was a slip of paper with the project's logo and a short, typed note: *We need to talk. Meet me in the conference room – Gordon.*

The conference room was inconveniently located on the deck below, which meant negotiating a stairwell in the rough weather. He hurried, struggling to maintain his balance as the ship lurched in the high seas. With the usual dim lighting, negotiating each step was a challenge, but finally he made it to the lower deck and walked along a passageway to the conference-room door. The handle turned and the door opened for him. No one was there. Oddly enough, the light was already on.

He rather impatiently settled down to wait. Time ticked by, and then suddenly the lights went out. He was plunged into total darkness all alone.

Jason was working at his desk when the lights went out. At first he thought it was just his stateroom, but the dark passageway conveyed a more sinister message, a major power outage at sea. He reflexively opted to get outside to sunlight. His living quarters were located below the weather decks, and he had to feel his way along the passageway, climb a set of stairs and then push open a metal door. It resisted his efforts but then fell open as the ship rolled.

The scene that confronted Jason magnified his concerns about the loss of electricity. The large rollers were now peaked with whitecaps that foamed toward the side of the ship. *Aladdin* was broadside to the seas, and waves were breaking over the rail and washing into his sneakers. As far as he could tell, he was the only person on deck.

Meanwhile, just before his lights went out Gordon was attempting another phone call to his office to join an emergency Board meeting. When the power was lost, the telephone also went dead. Gordon was seated on the sofa in the captain's cabin. Daylight illuminated the room so he wasn't plunged into darkness. He stared at the handset with growing irritation; he almost desperately needed input from his shore team. He got up to go to the bridge and find out when they might be able to reestablish satellite communications.

Just before lights went out, Captain Pearson had been focused on the ship's optimum track. Given the Sea State and the direction the waves were coming at the ship, he needed to make some concession to the weather and follow a dogleg to the California coast. The sudden power loss triggered a series of alarms all at once on the helm console. The bridge watch shouted to him: "Sir, we've lost steering control with the rudder at left ten degrees."

"Very well. Engines stop."

He moved fast to the sound-powered phone which connected key stations in the ship, and turned the crank to alert the engine room to an incoming call. In the short conversation that ensued, the Captain learned that the ship's main generator had tripped off-line and the emergency generator had failed to kick in.

On the bridge he realized that with the engines stopped and the ship now wallowing in the trough, he could be putting passengers at risk, so he gave the order to put the engines ahead one-third. *Aladdin* answered slowly, too slowly, so additional power was applied until the ship's bow was pitching into the oncoming seas. The ship's motion was now more predictable, and the ride became less turbulent.

Then the Chief Engineer was on the line to the bridge. "Captain, the symptoms look like the bushing on the main generator burned through. We're still investigating. If that's the problem, I'm not sure we can repair it while underway. Oh, and the emergency generator's circuit breaker was found open, so it never got a signal to start. We'll have emergency power in five minutes, but you need to tell all passengers not to use any equipment that would create a heavy demand for electricity, otherwise we might lose the emergency generator."

Several decks below, Aaron drummed his fingers impatiently in the darkness and cursed loudly. His first reaction had been to find his way in the dark to the door and get topside into sunlight, but the rolling deck discouraged him. And besides, he assumed the blackout was temporary. So he sat, letting his mind wander off to a beach in Connecticut where his wife and eldest grown son and his family were right now, enjoying the old vacation cottage where he could have been if he hadn't been so hard-headed and taken on this challenge.

The ship continued to wallow in ever-steeper seas, making walking anywhere on board very difficult and even dangerous in the dark. Which was why Aaron was surprised to hear movement in the passageway. Someone had been thrown up against the bulkhead next to the conference-room door.

Then silence, except for vague tiny sounds that Aaron started to imagine he was hearing. He even thought he heard the door open. He sensed rather than heard movement. The creepy feeling of no longer being all alone in the darkness gripped his breathing. He was almost ready, despite the non-stop tossing of the ship, to get up and feel his way to the door and somehow get topside. He had a visual image of the room, he felt confident that he could do it. The blackness was now threatening, surrounding him, closing in from all directions.

His arms and hands were resting on top of the table, when he felt something bump against it.

"What? Gordon? Is that you?"

There was no response.

He knew fear. "Hey, who's there?"

The only sound was the ringing and pulsing in his ears. Terror overwhelmed him. He sensed a definite presence looming somewhere in the void, its identity and motives entirely unknown.

And then the lights came on! And there was a man standing in front of him.

"Oh, it's you," Dr. Kline muttered at the man standing just three feet away. "Dammit, you scared me half to death!"

Then he saw the knife.

"But no! What?"

He watched stupefied as the lethal blade came fast at him. It disappeared under his chin, moving directly and quite surgically across his throat.

- 14 -

Jason's Theory

~~~~~~~~~~~~~~~~

The lights came on to a collective cheer from everybody who had gathered on the mess deck. On the bridge, Captain Pearson breathed a sigh of relief. Electric power meant he again had steering control. He immediately returned the ship to a more easterly heading. The track would avoid the worst of the trough but added about four hours to their expected time of arrival.

Professor Blake came storming up to the bridge. "Now what the hell caused that?" he demanded, masking his underlying fear.

"Not sure but I'm on it," Duke barked right back. "Could have been several things. I'll know soon enough."

"And where is Aaron?"

"Hey, I'm not keeping an eye on your team."

"Well, what if that electrical failure was sabotage too?"

The Captain spun around to face his old friend. "Gordon, are you losing your mind? Calm down."

"Just answer my question."

"Well, of course it could have been sabotage, somebody could have opened the emergency generator circuit so that it didn't cut in properly when the main generator failed. All I'm focused on right now is getting this ship to port. Any luck on your side?"

"That's why I'm looking for Aaron. He told me a few hours ago he was onto something."

"Something such as?" the Captain queried.

"He didn't say. And now he's missing?"

"Keep looking for another fifteen minutes. Then if he doesn't show, I'll call for a muster."

"Well okay." And Gordon stomped out of the pilot house.

Jason was also searching for someone, but Karen was seemingly elusive. He half ran down to her stateroom. No response. Was she sleeping? He pounded and shouted again, then took off to check the other places she was usually found. Control. Not there. Communications?

"Charlie, have you seen Karen?" he asked Hale, who was busy at his computer desk.

Charlie looked up, distracted. "No. What was that lights off all about? I always panic when the lights go out."

"Yeah, me too. We're basically lost out here without power. Look, I gotta run. Tell Karen I'm looking for her if you see her."

Charlie nodded. "Will do. She'll show. Unless she was out on deck and got washed overboard."

"She's too smart for that."

"Well good hunting," Charlie said to him as Jason hurried out of the room, slamming the door behind him.

He finally found her in a most unusual place, outside in a wind-sheltered nook, sitting alone with a blanket around her and a pillow under her. She looked up at him as he approached, then turned her head and stared again out to sea. He sat down cross-legged beside her. She didn't say anything.

"So, bit scary, lights off like that," he said to her.

She didn't reply.

"You okay?" he asked.

Again no response, but then she inhaled as if returning from some very distant inner place. "Oh," she said, barely audible. "Me okay? Maybe I'll never be okay again. I couldn't take being inside so here I am, stuck on this giant hunk of metal that can just instantly go dark. No, I'm not okay, I hate feeling trapped."

He was quiet for a moment. "I know. I think everybody on board right now feels just how fragile life is for us, way out here."

"I just want to get back to land. Humans, we think we can live anywhere, do anything. Right now I feel like at any moment the lights can go off for our whole species. We're so damn dependent on electricity! I mean at any moment a giant solar flare could hit us and blow out all the transformers and power grids and here'd we sit, in the dark. End of story."

"My doctoral research was on clarifying just how fragile each species on Earth is. We all have to live within such tight parameters of temperature, pressure, water, food. We're messing all that up, and at the same time there are creatures ten thousand feet below us right now who live on sulfur in radical heat. And we want to mess all that up too. Well, over my dead body."

"Don't say that! And be honest with me, Jason. Do you think the saboteur disabled the generator? I'm scared to death worrying about what he's going to do next. Why would he want us all to be marooned way out here?"

"Karen, you need to calm down."

"Calm down? Somebody tries to kill you, then they drop us into total darkness. They're still right here on board, and you want me to calm down?"

She paused, caught her breath. "Ever since your dive," she went on in a quieter voice, "I've been looking at faces, trying to see if it's him. Jason, I'm going slightly crazy. Thanks for finding me."

He said nothing. He put his arm around her and held her close to him. And then he felt her whole frame slightly shaking, silently convulsing with sobs.

"You're so cool and collected," she muttered at him. "You're so disciplined and courageous when you need to be, and so warm and kind and gentle otherwise, and you're amusing on top of it all. You're everything I'm not. I just feel totally empty and frightened and hopeless."

"Well when the lights came back on I went hunting for you because I felt just the same," he told her softly. "Ever since we kissed, I admit, you're on my mind all the time. And hey, you're intelligent, determined, caring, thoughtful – not to mention too darn beautiful for your own good. Who knows what's going on aboard this ship, but I need to tell you, Karen, that you are more important to me than anything or anyone I've ever known. The idea of you maybe being swept overboard drove me crazy."

She finally turned her head and looked into his eyes. There was no avoiding the kiss that followed, and it was more than a kiss of passion. They were bonding, two lovers in a world they can't control.

Finally she pushed back and spoke in a rush. "So now I must tell you something. When you went silent down there in the black deep, I started to go a little out of my head with all the waiting, the utter uncertainty of you still being alive, and somehow I went off into a random flow of thoughts and imaginations. And for no reason I found myself imagining taking you home to meet my family and you fitting in so beautifully ... and now, just telling you about that is really freaking me out. I gotta go."

She got up stiffly, grabbed pillow and blanket and hurried away, leaving Jason sitting there alone in the cold for several long minutes, trying to get a grip on the confusion of emotions surging through him. Was this really love? Really for the first time? And even if everything worked out for them, would there be a habitable world left to raise kids and have a family and future?

Jason's mind took off into his usual upsetting environmental doomsday thoughts about how all human beings have such tight environmental limitations. Things have to be just so, a temperate climate, not too cold, not too hot. And of course breathable air and unpolluted rivers and oceans. Everybody's stuck right here on the surface of this planet, he muttered to himself. We can't live way down in the oceans or up in the sky. And on top of all that, there are evil people everywhere, like the saboteur on board this vessel, people who provoke violence and destruction.

"Well," he grumbled to himself, "if there's a maniac on board trying to sabotage this mission, it's gonna be him or me."

Gordon interrupted his ruminations, stomping along the deck looking panicked. "Well here you are," he blurted. "Why are you off hiding out here? And where's Karen and Aaron? I've been looking for you guys everywhere."

Jason exhaled loudly and stood up. "Karen was just here. We were, well, talking. But Aaron? No idea. Did you check the lab? If he's on board we'll find him. If he fell overboard in this weather, there's no hope."

Captain Pearson was still on the bridge keeping an eye on the worsening weather when Jason and Gordon came hurrying into the pilothouse after fifteen more minutes of searching the ship for Aaron. They'd checked everywhere but the conference room. The door was locked.

"Duke," Gordon whispered, emotional, "we have a man overboard. Aaron isn't anywhere. No one has seen him since the lights went out, and that's over an hour ago. He must've gone out on deck and been swept away. It's hell out there. Turn this ship around. We gotta search for him."

The Captain just stood there for a moment. His expression looked ashen. "Over an hour ago? In this sea? And night falling? Hell, Gordon. If we turn around and steam back to where he might have gone overboard, it'll be dark. The reality is clear. There's no way we could find him, and the water is so cold he would drown in minutes."

"What? You're saying you won't even go look for him?"

"I'm saying he's gone if he went overboard. We can do a muster to confirm your suspicions, but I make these decisions. Right now let's do a complete search of the ship. There's still hope he just fell asleep someplace you haven't looked yet."

Jason saw Gordon's agitated expression suddenly collapse into despair. "No," he muttered. "This can't be."

"It sucks," Duke said roughly to him. But Gordon just stood there staring off into space. The Captain turned to Jason. "Take him to his stateroom. Call the doctor to give him a sedative, then put him to bed. I've seen that expression before. Shock. Now do as I say. Get out of here. I have work to do."

Jason did as he was told, wondering where Karen was. He offered to stay with the Professor, but Gordon said he wanted to be alone. Jason left him sitting on his bed, still stunned, waiting for the doctor.

Jason literally ran into Karen in the passageway. He got her up to date. She stood there a moment, shaken. "Oh Jason. How much worse can it get? A whole series of near misses, and now this tragedy! I'm sorry about how I left you on deck. Can there be any possible link between Aaron's disappearance and all the other things that have been happening?"

"Why would anyone want to kill Aaron?" Jason asked her. "And are you implying that the same guy who tried to sabotage the dive is also screwing around with this ship, even damaging the generator?"

"Why would anyone sabotage the ship if their intent is just to shut down our research? What if the Captain is the target? And what if someone is trying to sabotage Frontier Explorers?"

They made their way up two decks and found Duke in his cabin. He was just hanging up the telephone after a call to the engine room.

"Come in," he said.

Jason spoke quickly, "Captain, we have a new theory about what's been going on. We think that you and not the Professor may be the real target."

"You do, do you?" he retorted. But then his terse expression mellowed. "Well I just talked with the engineer and yes, somebody did tamper with the generator. So I've just reached the same conclusion. Is there anything else that I should know?"

"You probably heard that Charlie brought Gordon a message from our office verifying that none of the records we received were falsified. Gordon was trying to get the office again on the line but communication was down, and now he's out of it for the night."

"Why don't you use my telephone. If you don't have the number, get it, and come back." His face softened, and for the first time his glance took in Karen's presence. "You know, Jason, that you were in serious jeopardy down in the sub. This girl here ... she probably hasn't told you, but it's possible that you owe your life to her. She came up with ideas that saved your ass."

"What?" Jason said, surprised.

"Enough of that for now. Anything else?"

"No, sir. Thank you."

Karen spoke up. "Captain, you need to know. We might be able to isolate some of the messages on the LAN and trace signals sent to the submersibles back to their origin. If someone is screwing up the programs by using a remote computer, we might be able to find out who it is."

"So, what do you want?"

"Bert Hamblin left me with the impression that he could do that. Can you get him to cooperate with us?"

"Done. Now both of you, get to it. You're all I have. We're a team. Report regularly. Now I need to focus on getting this ship to port."

- 15 -
Hunter and Hunted
~~~~~~~~~~~~~~~~

Karen headed for Bert's office, and Jason returned to Gordon's stateroom to see how the Professor was doing and hopefully to obtain the telephone number for the office at the Scripps Institution. He was standing up, holding on to the bunk frame, and looking ill. "Gordon, why aren't you lying down? Did you talk to the doctor?"

"He came, but I won't take his pills, at least not yet. And as for lying down, are you serious? The way this ship is gyrating, I'd probably roll right onto the floor."

"Well the staterooms on my deck don't roll and heave as much as this one. They're down nearer the water and closer to the centerline. Let me get a crewmember to swap with you temporarily to sleep here. Come on, let's make the move."

And meanwhile, with the Captain's endorsement Karen was optimistic that Bert could open up files that would help pinpoint their man. After gaining access to the engineering spaces she found his cubicle – empty. And no one knew where he might have gone.

"Captain, here's another message from the office, again for your eyes only." Charlie delivered it personally.

"Thanks. Have a seat while I read it."

The message in fact substantiated his suspicions. It reported that Frontier Explorers was now conducting checks on a number of other employees based on some suspicious accidents aboard another one of their ships. When he had finished reading, Duke looked up at Charlie. "I want to bounce some things off of you."

The Captain quickly told him about Jason and Karen's suspicions about the real direction the sabotage effort appeared to be taking. "You seem to be sharp and even-tempered," he concluded. "And you're not in any of our suspicious circles. Plus you said you understand the LAN setup. Karen's theory that the messages would lead them to the saboteurs. Do you think she's right?"

"I couldn't say off-hand," Charlie said evenly. "But if you want, perhaps I could go assist her with her research."

"Ah, thanks, good. Get to it."

Jason got Blake as comfortably settled in his new quarters as could be expected under the circumstances. The older man lay down on the mattress, which was covered by a single sheet. Jason tucked in the second sheet and a blanket over him as tightly as he could, given the rolling and pitching deck.

"Listen," Jason said to him, "I do think you should take some light sedation and sleep. We're working with the Captain. Karen's into the LAN research and hopes to identify our man before daybreak."

"But … Aaron?" Blake's voice was now sounding very weak and distant.

"No info on him yet. We're still looking for him on board. Relax now, I'll have the doctor stop by here and give you something to ease your worry. Please, Gordon. Take it this time. We'll check back on you in an hour or so."

"You're a good man, Jason."

"Thank you sir."

When Jason got back to the bridge, the Captain hit him with a reality check. "It's my responsibility to report a missing person," he said. "I'll contact the appropriate authorities with just the basics. You'll need to inform the office and break the news to Gordon."

"I will. I expect the doctor is sedating him. Let's wait till tomorrow before we tell him what we think we know. I'm still hoping."

Karen was in her stateroom hunched over her computer when Jason appeared at her door. She looked up at him, her expression all business now.

"Any word on Aaron?" she asked evenly.

"Not yet."

"Well I thought it through and it just doesn't make sense that he would fall overboard, not after all the years he has spent doing research at sea. Why would he be so careless? It's not like him. The only other possibility is that someone pushed him, but if it's not any of us they're after, there's no motive. I'm at a loss."

"Yeah, me too. And both of us are dead tired."

"I must get back to work. I think I'm close."

"Well, I do have one new idea to check on. I'm going to find Derek and do a little sleuthing of my own."

He headed off down the passageway, his body feeling numb with fatigue but his mind racing. On the 02 level he entered the monitoring room. It was empty, which was understandable considering the time of night and the tossing of the ship. He eyed the video file boxes and decided to thumb through them to see if he could find what he was looking for without hunting for Derek.

On the next deck up, the watch could feel the ship buck underneath them when it pitched. Salt spume lathered the windows and then got blown away by the next gust of wind. The Captain visited the pilothouse to look at the barometer, read the forecast and review their track. Landfall would take place after sunset tomorrow.

Satisfied that they were doing all they could to reach the coast by tomorrow night, he returned to his cabin. The phone rang as he entered and closed the door behind him. It was the Chief Engineer.

"The good news is the initial generator diagnosis was incorrect. The bushing wasn't broken down. There had not been a short. But strangely, the sensors on the controls had responded as if there had been a short, so they must have received a spurious signal."

"But how the hell would that be possible?" Pearson demanded.

"I have no idea sir. We're looking into it while we also reassemble the generator."

"Well stay on it all night if you have to. Find out who or what caused the spurious signal – that's vital! And put a guard at the door. No one in or out except your core team until we're in port. Understood?"

Duke hung up the phone and walked through his cabin to the head to relieve himself. He remembered a Navy friend who called it recycling coffee. Such a normally simple bodily function is almost an art form in heavy weather. He braced his legs, grabbed a handrail next to the sink, and crouched slightly.

As he was standing there, he saw a face appear in the mirror, staring at the back of his head as he continued with his overdue pee.

"What are you doing in here? What's up? Something urgent?" he asked the man behind him.

The answer came in the form of a thin wire that was suddenly wrapped around his neck, so tightly that his breath was instantly cut off and the bleeding started. His knees buckled; his panic overcome as his life dwindled away.

So. The Captain had been easier than expected. The man smiled with satisfaction. Timing and precision, they were everything. Now he had to cover his remaining tracks quickly. He would finish the Professor and that brash young PhD in their staterooms – fast and clean. But he would ease up for just a few minutes and give himself a bit of well-deserved pleasure with the woman before he killed her. They all had to go. And after that, there would be no one at all who could be suspicious of him.

Jason's frustration was growing. The video files were numbered but not otherwise labeled, their contents a mystery. He hoped they would be in chronological order, but after viewing the beginning of four of them it was obvious that Derek or somebody had packed them away with no intention of referring to them again, at least not while at sea.

But Jason had to confirm the idea that had exploded in his mind thirty minutes ago. If the video revealed what he hoped it would, they would have their man, or at least one of them. He tried yet another video. No go.

He located the ship's phone and dialed the crew's lounge. The man who answered offered to find Derek and asked Jason to wait. While he stood in the middle of the empty monitoring room, Jason was suddenly aware of just how isolated he was and in a helpless ship in a hostile ocean. Whoever was at the bottom of all this had tried to kill him, but really, why? He could not escape thinking about Aaron. Was it possible he was murdered? And why him? Furthermore, if so, why *just* him?

"Derek."

"Derek. Jason. I need you here, right now."

There was a slight chuckle at the other end of the line. "Jason, I'm on my way, but *where* is *here*?"

He had no difficulty reaching the second deck and Jason's stateroom undetected. He relished the rough weather and was grateful for its cover. No one was moving about. Everyone had found some place to ride out the storm, and most would be in their bunks. Any noise he made in the passageway was covered by the wind and the metallic grinding sounds the ship made as it worked its way through the turbulent seas.

As he knew from his exploratory excursions, Jason's stateroom door was just aft of the ladder a few steps, which he took with cat-like grace over the moving deck. His right hand reached for the doorknob and closed around it, gripping it firmly before attempting to turn it noiselessly. Because the ship's movements were so unpredictable, he braced his other hand on the door jamb. His knife was sheathed in his pocket, a risk if Jason was alerted but accessible if required. The knob didn't turn, it was locked. Unusual for Jason. Pick it? No. On to Plan B. He hurried down passageways and up toward the Professor's quarters. Time was running out. Get this done!

Derek showed up promptly. The urgency in Jason's voice was compelling, and his curiosity, not to mention considerable concern, was written all over his face.

"Can you find one video file out of that lot, if I tell you what I'm looking for?" Jason said, not wasting any time on social niceties.

"If you give me a date and a time, sure."

"Okay. Do you remember the day we trialed the Bird? The day after the Professor and Karen got here?"

"Of course. I took that trip, remember?"

"So here's the deal. You told the informal inquiry that the cameras were working just fine before the launch. You knew they were because you had tested them by filming the handling crew on deck that morning. Can you find that video?"

Karen and Bert were playing similar games. Bert's first LAN file listed all the stations on the local net by location. It also contained a digital image of the ship's floor plan, deck by deck. The information thrilled Karen. If she could isolate messages by source to these spaces, and get a roster of who occupied them, she would be well on her way. She scrolled through the file quickly. The network supported four decks and several key stations deeper in the ship, mostly in the engineering spaces.

The next file answered her question as if she was in dialogue with the computer. Users on the LAN were listed alphabetically in a long column. The spaces they lived in and the spaces they worked in were listed in parallel columns on the right. Bert or someone had included a notation that indicated whether or not the space was online. Karen's heart was racing. Where was Jason?

He took the steps two at a time to the main deck. He knew exactly where he was going and what he had to do now. The Professor would present no challenge, locked door or not. He was almost beginning to enjoy this. He had been in equally dangerous circumstances numerous times in the past, and overcoming the odds was always thrilling. To finish an assassination and escape undetected and unidentified was the perfect crime, and he had numerous perfection-notches on his belt.

His approach to the door was similar to the procedure he used below, and this time the knob turned in his hand. As he rotated it slowly, he felt rather than heard the latch withdraw from its hole. The passageway was bathed in yellow light. No one had converted the ship's lighting for the night. That would present a small problem as the widening crack in the door admitted a beam of light into the sleeping man's room. The warning it would provide urged him to hurry. His training reminded him to take things one cautious step at a time. Experience said deal with both concurrently.

He eased into the room, glancing at the bunk to get his orientation. He'd seen the sleeping figure, lying on his side with his back to the intruder. The sleeper was entangled in his sheet – perfect.

Karen found that the third file was filled with network statistics concerning such things as overall usage, reliability, peak demand, and the amount of memory remaining. Karen closed it and clicked on file four. As she did so, an icon at the bottom of her screen started to blink. She ignored it, because file four was listed as information about the signals exchanged between the bridge and the engine room, a log of every order issued for speed and engine changes. She was hoping almost desperately that the file would also list messages between the ship and each of the submersibles.

The blinking icon irritated her. Hoping that by acknowledging it she could shut it off, she clicked on it and was jolted to find an email addressed to her. She gasped, and opened it.

"Karen. I'm in the computer room. I can see you logged in. I've traced the messages to the submersibles. You have got to see this. Be careful, the weather is still terrible. Jason."

The message was astounding. How had Jason ended up in the computer room? Is that what he was being so mysterious about? What did he know that she didn't yet? How did he get ahead of her? She clicked to acknowledge Jason's message and responded.

DEEP PERIL

"Jason, I'm coming. Karen."

- 16 -
Disaster
~~~~~~~~~~~~~~~~

She pressed her laptop closed and shut the desk to keep the computer from sliding off onto the deck. A random wave slammed into the hull, knocking her off her feet back into her chair. Timing the roll, she regained her feet, extricated herself from the chair and reached for the door. She looked to her left and right before entering the corridor. She was alone.

With the lights on, her effort to move aft would be significantly easier than the blind staggering journey she had made to reach the mess deck earlier that day. The starboard quarter would be relatively protected from the wind, and the seas would be rolling away from the hull. Mustering her resolve, Karen turned the exit-door handle. The door flew open, pulled free of her hand by the raging weather.

The deck was wet and glistened in the light from the interior. She could make out white caps surging from the ship. The deck rolled away from her and then leveled off, sloping into swells. Karen stood there in the gloom, clutching the handrail that ran along the deckhouse. Driven by sheer determination, she edged down the deck, facing the onset of rain and a light spray blowing over the ship to port. The wind gusted at her from different directions and her hair swirled around her face.

The thought that she was not alone out on deck never occurred to her. No one would be out here on a normal stormy night. The lights in the laboratory were on, shining out through the window. She hurried on her way toward the computer room entry, but on instinct turned to look behind and saw the vague figure of a man about fifty feet away.

Whoever it was, he was having the same difficulty negotiating the weather. His presence made no sense. Jason wouldn't have summoned anyone else. Karen's imagination flared as she panicked with the suspicion that the email had been false, that Jason was not in the computer room, that she'd been a fool. And she was in a trap.

"That's good, Derek. That's good. Stop the frame. Let's take a look." Derek had fast-forwarded the video through the equivalent of an hour and twenty minutes of pre-dive preparations, stopping periodically to confirm that the only people seen in the video were Jonas Pennypacker, Tom Ambrose, Billy Snow and Alberto Gomez. Then Jason had noticed an arm and shoulder which he couldn't account for. They both leaned toward the monitor.

"Shirt's different from the others. Looks like a golfer."

"Where would he have to be standing, to get in the picture like that?"

"He would be standing over by Trilobite."

"Hmm."

They worked through the video of four men working at high speed for the equivalent of another 45 minutes running time. Then one by one they disappeared off the screen. Derek pressed another button and the video player redoubled its speed. The clock on the monitor scrolled quickly. Then suddenly a figure passed through the camera field almost as a momentary discoloration.

Jason shouted for Derek to rewind the video. At the appropriate point he tapped 'play' and the same shirt they had observed earlier appeared, showing not a face but a torso that moved toward the camera, getting slightly out of focus before disappearing to the camera's left.

"Were you watching the camera at this point?" Jason asked impatiently.

"No. I had finished my checks and was getting myself ready for the dive."

They turned back to the monitor in the hope that whoever was wearing that polo shirt would reappear and they could get a glimpse of his face.

"He's back!" They both leaned into the monitor and studied the image. An arm and a sleeve appeared on the left. The camera was capturing a man at work, his muscles flexing with effort that was taking place out of sight. Then, the arm vanished, and shortly thereafter a crouching figure stared full face into the lens. "Freeze frame!"

Karen strained in the near darkness to make out what the man's next move might be. She began to tremble, and her fear angered her. Whoever he was, he was now unseen from her viewpoint. Surely even in this darkness she would see *something*. She backed away, clutching the handrail behind her, and worked her way past the crane. Her fingers encountered the security rope. She had forgotten the flimsy warning that had been rigged to keep all hands away from the submersibles.

As she ducked under the barrier and searched with her hands for the next handrail, she heard something bang with a metallic sound and then a soft curse. She gasped. Her pursuer sounded only a couple yards behind her. She gripped the rope and worked herself quickly through the wind and rain away from the deckhouse down toward the water. Then she paused and waited, blinded by the night, caught between a human predator and the roiling waves. Horrific seconds passed. She felt consumed by the wind and the rain and her terror.

The rope she was holding onto jumped suddenly. Whoever was there had reached the barrier. Karen let go of the line involuntarily and stepped away from it as if it had a current running through it. The ship took a deep roll that upset her balance. Her shuffling feet tripped over something on the deck, and she fell.

She landed on her back and shoulders and let out a yelp as she slid into the scuppers. She felt pain jabbing at her right shoulder, and she had hit her head on something hard. She felt utterly lost, hopeless, and started to whimper. Regaining her senses, she couldn't detect anything moving, and there was no noise from her pursuer. The blackness of the stormy night was imprisoning her. She considered screaming, but the only one to hear her would be her stalker, who hopefully didn't know exactly where she was.

"Charlie Hale? That doesn't make sense." Derek was confounded. "Who were you looking for?"

Jason looked grim. "Charlie Hale." The film confirmed what he had suspected ever since leaving Karen to do her research. The bogus email files could only have been altered in the communications room. It would have been easy to edit them and run them through the computer a second time. The 'message' from the headquarters now made sense because they had never sent it. Somewhere in the communications room was the real transmission, assuming there had been one and Charlie had not deleted it. And now they had evidence to show that he had also sabotaged the test dive.

Still glued to the screen, Jason was staring into the face of the man who had tried to kill him. They had been fortunate that his efforts hadn't killed anyone. The big question remaining in Jason's mind was Hale's motive. Who was this guy? Who was he working for?

"We've got to tell the Captain," Jason said, "and I'm going to wake the Professor."

The Captain's door was closed and locked. There was no answer, so they moved on to the bridge to see if he was there. The bridge bucked and rolled, keeping them constantly off balance. They had to shout their questions to the man in charge over the roaring sound of the wind.

"The Captain went to his cabin. I don't know why he doesn't answer the door," he responded. "He's probably in the head. I'll buzz him." He picked up the phone and called the Captain, but there was no answer. "Strange, the phone's accessible at his desk, his bunk, and even in the head."

He turned to the helmsman. "I'm going to the Captain's cabin, be right back."

At the Captain's door, the officer tried knocking, then took out a key and opened the door.

"Captain?"

No answer. Empty stateroom. Jason hurried ahead of the officer into the bathroom. Duke Pearson was curled up on the deck. His body had slipped into a fetal position, the rolling ship working him into a ball.

Karen lay unmoving, chilled to the bone with the seawater continuing to wash over her. She clutched at the lifeline just over her head and felt her grip weakening. She rolled over onto her stomach and pushed herself into a kneeling position. Rather than attempt to stand erect, she began to crawl on her hands and knees across the deck to a dryer place away from the surging water. The superstructure loomed ahead of her.

She realized that she had lost control of herself. As she struggled to overcome her panic, she felt a rising fury. Maybe physically she was no match for a man, but she was not going to allow herself to be driven overboard without a fight. Then just as she was summoning her courage, he emerged from the deeper darkness of the deckhouse, moving fast, and grabbed at her hair, yanking her violently forward.

Her involuntary screams disappeared into the windy night. Her assailant dragged her across the deck on her hands and knees. When they reached the bulkhead she tried to grab his wrist with both hands in an effort to free herself. His response was to twist her head into submission and lay the flat of a large knife blade along her cheek: "This knife just killed Blake," he hissed. "I'll gladly use it on you right now if that's what you want."

The cold steel and the chilling comment deflated her. She kneeled in front of him in a gesture of surrender, her hands hanging limply at her sides. She was sobbing. Her hair was still entangled in his fingers. To anyone who came upon them, the scene would have suggested the moment before a beheading.

He jerked her to her feet and tugged at her head to lead her toward the computer room. Karen didn't know where she was until he ordered her to open the door and the light assaulted her eyes. He pushed her through the opening and extracted his fingers from her hair. She stumbled forward and then turned to face him.

"Charlie!"

"For purposes of this cruise that name will do."

Karen was terrified as he circled her and moved closer. Her eyes were wide with fear as she backed away from him and banged into an equipment cabinet. He was so close she could smell cigarettes on his breath.

"What? You killed the Professor? Are you totally crazy?" she growled at him.

He responded rather matter-of-factly, "Doctor Kline, the Captain *and* the Professor."

She felt shame at her relief that he hadn't mentioned Jason. As if reading her thoughts, he continued. "Jason lucked out. If I had found him, I wouldn't be making such a dramatic exit. There wouldn't be anyone to implicate me. My, you are a beauty. I've wanted you from the day you came on board."

He held the knife at her neck, pricking her slightly with the point. She felt her body give way, she almost fainted. And when he forced his mouth onto hers, she began to weep. She could feel his excitement; he was aroused by her submission. His tobacco mouth on hers and his free hand groping her so disgusted her that she involuntarily pushed him away.

He laughed. "A little fight in a woman – I like that. But too much fight and I'll start cutting things off."

He yanked a keyboard cable free and pushed her down onto the deck on her stomach, grabbing her all over in the process and enjoying every moment as he roughly wrapped the cable around her wrists behind her back. In that sexually vulnerable position she feared the worst, but he just took another cable and tied her ankles.

"When I untie you, I imagine you'll do just about anything I want, and I mean anything. But right now I need to take care of a few final things."

The discovery of the Captain's obviously murdered body had sent the watch officer into utter confusion. He was technically the second in command, but Pennypacker was the one who had the experience and leadership to deal with this crisis. He was called to the bridge. Word was passed over the ship's loudspeaker system for all hands to assemble on the mess deck.

When Pennypacker got to the bridge and learned that the Captain had been murdered, he took no time reaching the conclusion that he needed help. This crew was not equipped to deal with a killer. He called the Coast Guard and asked for an armed team to embark as soon as they could get to the ship.

Jason took Derek aside. "We've got a maniac on board. We need to find the Professor and Karen right now. You look for Karen. I'll get Gordon. We'll meet on the mess deck." Jason told Derek four primary places to look for Karen, and then took off for his own stateroom where Gordon should be sleeping.

Jason pressed on in the opposite direction that all the passengers and crew on board were taking to the mess deck. Some asked him if he knew what was going on, but he offered no response. Rushing to his stateroom, he found it locked. When he unlocked and opened the door, the interior light was on, and Blake was standing up in the middle of the room looking disoriented.

"Gordon, I have a lot of bad news."

The Professor looked resigned to tragedy. "I can guess. You haven't found Aaron."

Jason wasted no time trying to frame a gentler response. "The search has been abandoned. It's night. The storm is still raging. No hope."

"Oh mercy. I must call his wife. She needs to hear it from me. Where's a telephone?"

"Sir, there is more. Do you want to sit down?"

Blake was summoning strength from some inner source. "No, hit me with it."

"The Captain is dead. Someone killed him in his stateroom. About an hour ago. The murderer is on the loose. This is an absolute emergency, and we need you. We are assembling on the mess deck. Let's go."

"The Captain? Duke? Dead?"

"Yes, and very possibly Charlie Hale did it."

Derek appeared breathless at the door. "No sign of Karen – she's missing."

For the second time in fifteen minutes the loudspeaker system called for attention. "The following people must call the bridge or appear on the mess deck immediately: Gordon Blake, Karen Finch, Charlie Hale, Tom Lassiter and Richard Greenberg."

Jason didn't know the fourth name, probably a sailor, but the fifth name was his colleague who had switched rooms with the Professor for the night. Jason turned to Gordon, "It's not safe for you here. I'll send Derek to take you to the mess deck. I'll go find Karen." And without waiting for a response he took off on the run.

Charlie was working fast at the computer. He had logged in, using passwords that only the SYSAD should have known. Karen had her head turned and could see him working. She struggled to summon her voice.

"Charlie, this is insane. What are you doing now?" she asked, trying to muster some strength to her tone.

"Oh, just sending messages to remote stations in the engine room. You and Jason were such pests, I've been forced to abandon plan A. Damn shame, I did so much plotting and, well, adjusting. It would have worked quite perfectly. No one would have guessed anything except for you nosing around."

"But you seemed so – so normal."

He glanced at her. "Oh yes," he sneered, "I can appear utterly normal when needed."

"Why are you doing this? What are you hoping to gain?"

"Oh. That's easy. Money. Revenge. Freedom."

"You would kill just for money? You'll rot in hell forever!"

"No. No. The truth is I'll live the rest of my life in perfect preplanned paradise."

"You're never going to get off this ship. You can't kill people and expect to escape."

"That's why I have Plan B. Just wait, and see. Who knows, I might even take you with me. I do believe there's room for two. But quiet! I need to time all this just right. *Aladdin* will go down mysteriously by the stern, and I shall literally slip away. Now shut up, or I'll shut you up right now!

Jason reached Karen's room. The door was unlocked and her lights were on, but the space was unoccupied. He hurriedly looked around for any clues of her whereabouts. To his relief, there were no signs of violence, but she had left no messages to help him find her.

Then he opened her desk and found her laptop. It was still on. She must have left in a hurry. What or who could have provoked her urgent departure? Desperate, he tapped the screen. There was a message 'to Jason' from Karen, staring up at him. He moved the cursor to recent incoming messages and discovered the bogus email sent from the computer room. Someone had called for her, and it hadn't been Jason.

As he studied the screen a loud alarm sounded in the passageway. He recognized it as the Fire and Flooding Alarm they had sounded for drills during the first day underway. Spurred into action, he went running as fast as he could up to the mess deck where the fire alarm had summoned everyone who had no designated emergency duties.

Below, the firefighting team quickly assembled outside of the engineering spaces at the equipment locker. The lead engineman summoned his nerve and disappeared into the forward engine room, narrating what he saw and felt to the team leader by a radio embedded in his helmet.

In the computer room, Karen had fallen silent. Charlie was watching the engine room signals with fascination. If the crew had already figured out that there was no fire, they still hadn't done anything to turn off the fire pumps. The first one had come on in response to his signal, activating the sprinklers in the aft engine room. When the water pressure failed to reach a useful level in the fire main, the next pump would automatically kick in. Already hundreds of gallons were pouring into the bilge. Normally a set of pumps would drain it as it flooded, but he had already disabled them.

Having seen enough, Charlie turned his attention to Karen. Her face was white with pain, there would be no fight left in her. He pulled out his knife and approached her. She showed no signs of resistance.

"Chief, this is Investigator One. I am not seeing any smoke, and the ambient temperature is seventy-eight degrees. I am at the aft bulkhead preparing to enter Number Two Engine Room."

The Chief Engineer nodded, and the message on the speaker was acknowledged. He was getting suspicious. The first fire pump was on-line, and the pressure in the main was not climbing. Conditions in the forward engine room didn't make sense either. The temperature for the space was normal. A fire in an adjacent space ought to be driving it up.

"Chief, the bulkhead between the engine rooms is cool. Have I permission to enter the space?"

"Tell him permission granted, but he is not to proceed any farther than the door. I want to know what he sees."

Just as the Chief Engineer finished giving these orders, the second fire pump started. Pressure spiked briefly before settling back into a range that would soon automatically activate the third pump. As the investigating team approached the door to the aft engine room, the pumps were flooding the space. Salt water sloshed around the engine mounts and in another two feet, it would disable the engine.

The third pump came on as the investigating team prepared to open the door. They assumed the water level was climbing rapidly. This was clearly a crisis. Most of the auxiliary equipment and the main engine would be engulfed in swirling water from the high-pressure discharge. The ship at this rate would soon start to sink.

Charlie cut the cord around Karen's wrists and ankles. He could see her watching him through wet strands of her hair. He moved the strands from her face with the tip of his knife.

"Indeed you're a beauty," he said to her. "Such a pity we won't have time for everything I've been imagining doing to you."

He roughly rolled her over onto her back and spread her legs and let his fingers grab and prod her body everywhere he wanted. Then he plunged his knife blade into its scabbard and worked fast to release his belt buckle.

- 17 -

Survival

~~~~~~~~~~~~~~~~

The investigator reached the bulkhead watertight door. He lifted the lever to release eight fittings simultaneously around its perimeter. The door burst open with a gush of seawater, knocking the firefighter off his feet. There was no time for a report but the helmet video camera conveyed the catastrophe that had overcome him.

The fourth fire pump came on, and the Chief Engineer fully recognized the magnitude of the situation. He gave orders to secure the pumps. It was possible that they could reverse the disaster, but the survival of the ship depended on how fast they could control the flooding. *Aladdin* was without propulsion. Listless in the storm, its rolling now increased.

And for no known reason the pumps simply would not turn off. Repeated signals to them provoked no response. Having taken command of the ship, Pennypacker called the Coast Guard to report that, based on the latest report from the Chief Engineer, the ship was on the verge of sinking – with the lives of forty-five, or more correctly now forty-three, people on board at stake.

Number one and number two fire pumps were shut down manually. The other two were out of reach.

The drain pump in the forward engine room was operating, but all these efforts were not enough. Flooding now threatened the forward engine room as water continued to rise and pour through the open door. The aft engine room was evacuated and sealed, but the two remaining fire pumps continued to slowly fill *Aladdin*.

On the bridge Pennypacker got a phone call from the Coast Guard. "We've dispatched a helicopter with an emergency pump and federal law enforcement officers. They will arrive at first light, and there's a cutter enroute to your location."

His morale rose another notch when the quartermaster reported that the wind had dropped in the last hour. But his hopes got squashed by another report from below from the Chief Engineer. "We are still flooding. I have sealed off both engine rooms, but to shut down the pumps I must cut electrical power aft. You will lose steering, but not the bridge communications equipment and the navigation lights."

"Roger. Do what you must." *Aladdin* was adrift with the long steep seas breaking over her stern and washing up the main deck. He tried to weigh the odds of the vessel's survival and then began to consider what preparations must be made to abandon ship.

"Let go of her, you bastard!"

Jason had appeared at the door. Charlie had Karen down in the water, groping at her. She had just kneed him hard in the groin, and he was enraged. Hearing the raw howl, he looked up at Jason, threw Karen to the side into the moving slush of sea water, and stood up unsteadily to face Jason.

"Ah, perfect timing," he muttered. "I'll kill both of you." As Jason came lunging toward him he reached for his knife and drew it from its scabbard.

The overhead lights went out, leaving the room in a vague weird light from the computer bank, drawing on its battery power.

Jason had grabbed a dogging wrench from somewhere outside as a weapon, and he was eager to use it on his adversary. As Charlie's knife slashed through the air, aimed at his throat, a sudden ocean surge shifted the deck. Charlie stumbled, and Jason delivered a hard blow to the base of his head. Charlie crumpled into the water at the doorway.

Jason splashed into the middle of the room, tripped over Karen's leg, and fell sprawling in the inky water. Karen thought he was Charlie. She had recovered enough to pounce on his body and try to push his face into the water to drown him.

Jason struggled, "Karen, stop! It's me!"

She rolled off his back, and sat upright in six inches of swirling water, confused and relieved by his presence. Except for the wind whistling past the door and the sound of water sloshing under the equipment mounts, the room was suddenly perfectly still. Jason could see her ghostly silhouette and now he heard her sobs. "Where is he?" she muttered. "I'll kill him!"

"I think he's gone. We can't stay here. The water's still rising, and Charlie might come back. Do you think you can walk?"

"Do I have a choice?"

"Atta girl."

He helped her to her feet. She wrapped her arm around his waist, and they staggered toward the dark hole of the door. But suddenly there was Charlie, rising directly in their path. He'd lost his knife, but he was bent on killing both of them. He lunged at Jason and hit him hard in the solar plexus, knocking him back and down. He grabbed Karen and toppled into the water with her.

Jason came up coughing gasping for air. He stood up and over to the two bodies writhing at his feet. He smashed Charlie's head with his fist and pulled Karen out from under him to get her head above water before she drowned. Charlie kicked him in the groin, and Jason staggered back and fell again.

Charlie was in a total rage. He grabbed Karen's neck with the intent of crushing her trachea. Jason was crawling toward them through the water, almost sobbing in pain but determined to perform a rescue. Charlie saw him coming and drove his elbow into Jason's face, knocking him almost senseless.

Karen, temporarily free from his grip, tried to make a splashing move away from him, but he threw her face-down again into the water, forcing her head under. Jason, dizzy from the elbow blow but somewhat conscious, forced himself into a sitting position. As he did so his left hand brushed over the lost wrench. He closed both of his fists around the handle and swung the weapon hard into Charlie's back.

He shrieked, released his grip on the back of Karen's head, and scrambled to get away from the next blow. He rolled off of Karen and stood up, staggering from the blow to his kidneys. Karen arched her back and moved both arms under her, gasping for air.

Charlie reached the port door and disappeared into the dark gale.

- 18 -
The Search

~~~~~~~~~~~~~~~~

Fear pervaded those on the mess deck while the engineers struggled to pump out the engine rooms. The absence of light thwarted their efforts below decks in a ship still taking on water. No one knew if the ship could be saved. The passengers huddled together, knowing that the Captain had been murdered by someone who was still at large somewhere on the ship.

"Bridge, this is the Chief Engineer. We are rigging to dewater number one engine room."

Pennypacker acknowledged the message without emotion. The news was promising. The pumps were off, and the water presumably no longer rising. If they could keep *Aladdin* afloat for just a few more hours they'd be able to make her seaworthy. Daylight would bring the helicopter and an additional pump. There was nothing he could do now but watch the clock.

"*Aladdin*, this is Coast Guard Cutter *Dauntless*. Over."

The radio volume had been turned up. Those within earshot jumped at the unexpected noise. "Coast Guard Cutter *Dauntless*, this is *Aladdin*. Over."

"*Aladdin*, *Dauntless*. We are enroute. What is your condition? Over."

"Sinking by the stern, but we've stopped the flooding in the engine rooms. Not sure whether we can save her. Over."

"Roger. We are sixty miles from your position making best speed. Estimate rendezvous at first light. Coast Guard helicopter side-number two-one-three will be enroute to your position at dawn with assistance. Over."

"Many, many thanks. We'll call you if conditions change." In Pennypacker's mind that meant 'if conditions worsen.'

Just then Jason and Karen, a slouching pair of water-logged fighters looking like death warmed over, appeared at the pilot house door. "Listen to me," Jason said to Pennypacker, "Charlie Hale is the one who killed Captain Pearson. He likewise tried like hell to kill us. He must be found before he kills anyone else or further sabotages the ship."

Gordon appeared on the bridge. Karen was so relieved to see him alive that her eyes started to fill with tears. "Oh, thank God," she said to him. "Charlie said he killed Aaron and the Captain – and you!"

Jason repeated what he had just told Pennypacker, and as they conferred, Pennypacker took charge. "Please," he said, "you look terrible, both of you. Go down and change into dry clothes. I'll order an armed search."

Gordon, Jason, and Karen filed down the passageway to the Professor's door. As Gordon put his hand on the knob, Jason remembered that his colleague would likely be sleeping there. Gordon entered first, turning on the light and then grunting with horror. There was blood all over the bulkhead behind the bed. The victim lay under red-stained sheets.

He turned to Jason and Karen. "Stay out," he muttered. "I'll phone the bridge."

Pennypacker listened to the dire news and then gave appropriate orders to his armed search teams. "Keep everybody together on the mess deck," he said. "Place guards at the lifeboats so Hale can't escape the ship. Then please, take your time, check every nook and cranny. Be careful. And be prepared to shoot him if he's armed or attacks."

He then called the Chief Engineer. The news from the decks below was good. The pumps were slowly gaining, and every gallon over the side improved *Aladdin's* chances of survival. Also the barometer was rising, and the wind was continuing to abate. Clouds were breaking up. Gaps in the cover were illuminated by ethereal light from the waxing crescent moon.

Charlie felt certain that under other circumstances he could have taken down the young inexperienced man. However, there had been two of them, and now he was in pain from the blow to his head and the blow to his back. Time was rapidly running out for Plan B. He'd adequately disrupted the research and would therefore receive his payment. That would be acceptable compensation, even if he didn't get the girl and kill her lover.

And the ship was slowly sinking as planned. The tilt of the deck was almost correct for the sub, once untethered, to slide off into the depths with just slight purposeful provocation. The actual sinking of the ship and the elimination of its passengers would just be frosting on the cake.

He stepped out onto the deck into the sloshing water and headed aft. The wind further chilled his soaked skin. He knew he needed to deal with that quite soon, but the rolling seas urged him to focus on his escape. The waves weren't climbing as far up the deck as they had been before. Hopefully this last phase of Plan B would go smoothly with no more bad luck. Who could have known that the pressure seal on the submarine could be repaired on board, or that the sled would be so resilient to his tampering? Who would have guessed that that damn woman would be smart enough to use the sub's black box to spotlight his ability to reprogram the submarine?

This whole mission reminded Charlie of an assassination gone wrong. He'd been in tight spots like this before, and killing to cover his tracks wasn't new to him. He pushed himself to overcome his wounds, moving aft past the winch room into water that was now knee deep. He was forced back several times by wave surges but finally reached the rigging that secured the submarine to its cradle.

The deep water was reassuring. The cresting waves would facilitate his next step. He started releasing the fittings that kept the sub from shifting. He circled the cradle as far as he could go, leaving just one final fitting in place to prevent the sub from sliding off the deck like a beached whale. He intended to have the Bird wash overboard, but only after he was inside with the hatch sealed.

The sub shifted slightly again in his direction. The sky was now brightening to the east, and the submarine loomed right over his head. Behind him he noticed several flashlights working their way down the deck. They would likely not pause to inspect the submersibles, but the beams from their lamps might catch him as he climbed up to board the sub. He backed out of their sight to see what they would do. He didn't have to wait long. They reached the computer room and disappeared inside. Time for action.

He climbed up onto the wing, then managed to work his way up the side of the sub to where the top surface was fairly flat. He grabbed the tether as the ship heaved and rolled. The submarine moved just slightly with the surge, edging it down the gently sloping deck. Charlie crawled as quickly as he could to the hatch tower. As he expected, the hatch was sealed. He would have to stand up precariously to work it open.

The Bird shuddered as a swell slammed into it. Hale's feet slipped out from under him, forcing him to his knees. He gripped the hatch and worked at it as he attempted to regain his feet. Pulling at the fitting with his right hand, he felt the seal break free.

The sub lurched again. Hale stepped over the seal and descended into the darkness, pulling the hatch closed behind him.

"Captain, we have completed the search of the chain locker, anchor windlass room, and the forward crew berthing area. There is no sign of Hale. Team Two has finished checking the spaces below. We're going to move aft and do all the spaces amidships next."

Pennypacker thanked him and hung up the phone. He envisioned a bloody fight with Charlie if and when they found him, and the news that so far they had had no success was actually a relief. They had a long way to go, however, to complete the search. He had to be somewhere if he wasn't overboard and lost at sea. In the meantime the forward engine room was draining. The survival prognosis was good.

Karen asked Jason to stand outside her door while she changed into dry clothes. She shut it, then opened it a crack to assure herself that he was still there.

"You're not going to get changed if you keep checking up on me," he assured her.

"I'm not checking up on you, Jason. I'm just so afraid to be alone."

Jason studied her tired, bruised, and frightened face through the crack in the door. Then he opened the door and reached for her, pulling her into a soft comforting hug. She shivered, then grabbed him and held him tightly against her.

Finally she pushed gently back. "Thank you. Thank you. So now let me try getting into dry clothes again."

They needed company and joined the press of people on the mess deck. Word was already circulating about their encounter with Charlie, and they were greeted with looks of admiration and curiosity. Derek crossed to meet them, gave each of them a hug, and led them to Gordon's table.

Jason asked Derek rather urgently: "Do they have any idea where he is?"

"They're searching the ship, working from bow to stern. Pennypacker has all exterior doors locked or guarded."

Suddenly the mess deck was stirring. One of the search teams had found Doctor Kline's body. Another death. Another murder. As the implications sunk in, the room fell into an eerie silence.

In spite of his exhaustion, Jason was pacing the deck, unable to hold still. Then he suddenly stopped pacing, pivoted on his heel, and faced the Professor.

"The sub," he blurted out. "Has anyone gone out and searched the Bird?"

Derek was not buying it. "Jason, even if he could get inside the sub, what's the point? It's a dead-end. He'd be trapping himself."

"Well he's not trapped if no one thinks to look for him there. Let's talk to Pennypacker and get out there."

- 19 -

Sunrise

~~~~~~~~~~~~~~~~

On the bridge, Pennypacker had just received a report from the Chief Engineer that the forward engine room water level was under control, but the space wasn't fully dry. Slow progress, but the operative word was 'progress.' The wind still punched at the windows in bursts, but the blows were weaker.

"*Aladdin*, this is Coast Guard Cutter *Dauntless*. Over."

Pennypacker hustled across the pilothouse to respond. "This is *Aladdin*. Over."

"*Aladdin*, we have you on radar. Will join you in just over one hour."

"We have three, repeat three, deaths on board. We are dewatering the ship, and it now appears we will save her. Over."

There was a pause, then another voice spoke over the phone. "This is Captain John Kramer. We will provide whatever support you need."

"Sir, we have a killer on board. He is unlocated. Request an armed boarding party if conditions permit."

"We will transfer a three-man team to you in the first boat."

Just as the conversation ended, a figure came rushing onto the bridge. "Pennypacker, I think I know where Hale is hiding."

"Jason. I thought you'd be asleep by now. You've had a tough night. We'll have an armed team boarding within the hour. Besides, how can you know where to find him when three teams haven't turned up a trace?"

"They've been looking in the wrong places! Charlie Hale left us in the computer room and headed aft. My bet is he's in the Bird. It's the only place outside the superstructure that's safe and dry – and out of sight."

Pennypacker took his time before responding. "The Coast Guard will be here soon with people equipped to deal with situations like this. Hale can't get back into the ship, so let's ease up for now."

"Are you serious? You're just going to let him sit there? You're not going to nail him?"

"He probably has a weapon. Let's let the Coast Guard handle this."

Charlie sat up against the bulkhead in the darkened submarine. He considered turning on a light but thought better of it. A light from one of the ports would arouse suspicion and draw a posse. The ship and sub lurched as a wave pounded the transom. He felt the sub slip its way a little farther aft. It would be only a matter of minutes before the sub went over the edge of the deck and dropped into the awaiting sea where he could engage the propeller and get away to safety.

Jason left Derek with Pennypacker on the bridge. He was frustrated and angry. Pennypacker was wrong, if not a coward. He descended to the mess deck and found Karen under a blanket, asleep on a bench the crew had cleared for her. He leaned over her. She looked like a little girl, breathing slowly and evenly, her arms tucked under her head, a wisp of hair stuck to her lips.

"Karen?" She did not move – but her eyes opened.

"Jason, what?"

"I think I know where Charlie is."

The words produced an immediate reaction. She came to life, sat up and stared at him. "Do you *think* or do you *know*?"

"There's only one place he can be – the Bird. After all, who would think to look there?"

Karen's eyes widened. "Oh my word, Jason, he's not hiding there, he's escaping! We've got to stop him!"

She got to her feet stiffly. Jason grabbed her right arm as the ship lurched, and they took off, working their way down the lighted passageway to the outside aft door. Except for a warning that Jason and Karen wouldn't be allowed back in without Pennypacker's okay, the two sailors guarding the door offered no objection.

Once on deck, it was clear that the storm was passing. The rain had stopped, and the clouds were being chased off by the remnants of the wind. In the rising light they could see deep swells which no longer crested. The ship was still wallowing in the long rollers that overtook *Aladdin* from aft, but they didn't climb up the deck as far as they had before.

"Jason, look! How are we going to reach the sub? It seems to have slipped."

And indeed the sub was now perched over the transom, hung up on the tiny deck edge, lifting and falling in the rolling water but not yet tumbling free. Jason studied the layout, looking for a way to reach the sub. Seeing none, he turned and ran over into the computer room. Karen ran after him.

"What are you doing?" she shouted at his back.

"Calling Pennypacker. We need help!"

He got the bridge on the phone, shouted at whoever answered it, then slammed down the phone.

"Damn," he growled at Karen. "He won't talk to me. He ordered me to the bridge. We could lose Charlie in the meantime."

Karen grabbed the phone off the cradle and called the Chief Engineer. When someone answered, she shouted at them with an urgency that she genuinely felt. "This is Karen Finch. I'm on the fantail. The submarine has broken loose, and it's opening a hole in the deck. We're going to have a terrible leak if you don't get some people up here immediately to tie down the sub!"

She hung up. Jason smiled in total admiration.

Karen and Jason waited by the door to the computer room, anxiously watching the submarine teeter on the edge of the deck.

"Look!" Karen shouted, pointing off to sea.

The Coast Guard cutter was cresting a wave, its white hull with its broad red stripe making good headway through the waves.

Soon thereafter a small team of panting sailors led by Derek came running up to them. "What's going on? Where's the hole?"

"No questions," Jason barked back. "Look! Do something, or the sub's going over."

Jason shouted at them. "Get the heavy manila line out of the winch house. Run it aft and secure the sub by its wings. And get a winch operator up here. Charlie Hale is in the Bird. Don't let him get away in the sub."

But too late. A big swell hit the ship, and the submersible lifted just enough to pitch over and off the deck. Cocking slightly sideways, the sub's starboard wing rose in a gesture of farewell. Everyone on deck stood helplessly mute as the yellow hull splashed into the water, bobbed just once, and then disappeared.

Jason muttered, "Damn, he got away!"

"No, Jason," Derek said, "he didn't get away. He's trapped, and he's probably going to die."

Karen and Jason looked at Derek in disbelief. "What do you mean?" Karen asked him.

"It's simple. In anticipation of our return to port at Simson's direction I disengaged the battery packs before the weather got really bad. I didn't have time to offload the ballast too. He has no propulsion, no lighting, and no communications. By now he knows that. And there is nothing he can do."

Those who heard what Derek had said stood there in stunned silence. One by one they turned to look at the water. The submarine would be descending hopelessly through the dark, falling like a pebble in a well, passing creatures that would attempt to dazzle the passing visitor as he made his first and only dive to the sea floor. Ten thousand feet below.

It would likely take Charlie Hale, or whatever his real name was, an interminable week to die, assuming the hull didn't implode upon impact with the bottom.

- 20 -
Resolution

~~~~~~~~~~~~~~~~

USCGC *Dauntless* slowly circled the ship to inspect it before heaving to within three hundred feet of *Aladdin's* port bridge wing. Her crew lowered a small rigid inflatable boat, and six men embarked to attend to the stricken ship. The coxswain was not carrying a weapon, but the others wore body armor and carried side arms. The team leader had seen the submarine pitch off the deck, but the significance of its loss was not yet appreciated.

Pennypacker was waiting for them at the top of the Jacob's Ladder. A young officer in dark blue coveralls called up to him. "Good morning, Captain, I'm Lieutenant Stuart. My Commanding Officer has told me you have a man on board who is armed and dangerous. Where do you think he is now?"

The short answer begged a long explanation. Captain Pennypacker escorted the Coast Guard detachment to the mess deck and briefed them on the events that had taken place during the past 36 hours. Arrangements were made to remove the corpses to the cutter and to transfer additional pumps to *Aladdin*, but because the helo was inbound, nothing would be done until it landed on the flight deck.

The Jayhawk helicopter checked in ten minutes later and appeared on the horizon shortly thereafter. The rising sun beamed through breaks in the cloud cover. The wind had dropped, and the long swells had abandoned their white caps. The view from the air revealed a reassuring picture. *Aladdin's* fantail was no longer awash.

Once the Jayhawk was secured on deck, *Dauntless* began to transfer men and equipment to *Aladdin*. If propulsion could not be restored, the cutter was prepared to tow them. In the meantime, the crew and passengers dispersed to their quarters to prepare for arrival. Gordon and Pennypacker, however, were closeted in the monitoring room with four new visitors.

When the first request for help had reached the Coast Guard, they called the Professor's office. The consortium had been on the brink of terminating the research project because they were alarmed by Gordon's request for background checks on his people. The Coast Guard's report clinched the decision and prompted them to notify the Federal Bureau of Investigation. The Navy was asked to effect a search and rescue mission in the deep. They quickly picked up on the emerging tragedy. As a result, the flight manifest included Dan Post, representing Frontier Explorers, Agent Walter Newman, FBI, and Captain Gilbert Paul, United States Navy. The fourth man, a civilian named Petersfield, had an impressive ID card but would not reveal what agency he worked for.

The Coast Guard law-enforcement team had examined every space on the ship, confirming that Charlie Hale was no longer on board. Captain Paul wanted details concerning the loss of the submarine and chafed under the implicit consensus among the others to concentrate on the escape. He left to make an initial report to his seniors, which started a chain of events that would lead to a major West Coast search and rescue attempt. The Captain returned soon.

The discussion moved quickly through the events of the past eight days. Dan Post took the lead, while the mysterious civilian listened impassively. When the recap was complete, Dan said bluntly, "Gordon, we have been the victim of industrial sabotage. You really hit a nerve with this summer project. Frontier Explorers has been gaining a commanding position in deep sea mining and biotechnology through their alliances with people like you and organizations like the Scripps and Woods Hole Institutions."

And now we have the Navy. He looked over at Captain Paul as if he were the entire Department, and continued. "Frontier Explorers owns the best database on Earth concerning the ocean floor. We have worked with governments around the world and with every major player in the United States. A lot of people would do anything to take us down. When you acquired the use of the submarine produced by Ocean Ventures and devoted that technology to explore the sea floor, you fueled a rivalry already ignited by greed."

He turned to the FBI agent. "The sea floor is going to be at least a multi-billion dollar bonanza. Is it any wonder that someone would elect to level the playing field using whatever means at his disposal? Gordon, *you* weren't the target, your project was."

Gordon stared at him blankly, unwilling to accept that the murders and sabotage could be explained away so matter-of-factly. "So then, tell me who did this to us?"

Petersfield spoke up. "You'll find out in due time. We are treating this as a national security issue. I can't tell you more."

Gordon started to protest, and Dan put up his hand. "Gordon, trust me. He's serious. I've already been down that road. It won't do you any good to press. The fact that we have three murder victims, though, will mean that this will get a lot more daylight than this gentleman is willing to give us now."

Petersfield ignored the comment and redirected the conversation to the subject of Charlie Hale. In doing so, he left them ignorant of the fact that two other major projects supported by Frontier Explorers were in jeopardy, a seabed research project with the Japanese off the Pacific Coast of South America and a South Atlantic fisheries data collection effort for a European consortium. In each case, sabotage had led to injuries but not death.

"Captain Pennypacker, assuming that we can at some point perhaps recover the submarine, we will get the details from its occupant. But what can you tell me about the man who called himself Charlie Hale?"

Pennypacker looked at his inquisitor, feeling intimidated by the man. "I'm not really the Captain. That was Duke Pearson. I don't know much about Hale, only that he was hired by the company and reported to Captain Pearson. I didn't work with him. He kept pretty much to himself. I ..."

Petersfield impatiently cut him off. "Thank you, Captain. The fact is that he *wasn't* Charlie Hale. There is, or rather was, such a man. We found his body in a ditch miles from the San Diego Airport. Your communications officer was a man named Stark, Michael Stark, although he often operated under the alias Walter Meyers. Yale graduate. Former Navy Seal. A jack of all trades. His willingness to do the more distasteful jobs made him valuable within a certain element of his community. Whether he was considered reckless or courageous, that's someone else's call.

"Stark operated on the edge all the time. His private life's a mess. His first wife, a Miss Virginia runner-up no less, left him, claiming he beat her. He was arrested twice on rape charges, but the victims refused to testify against him. Eventually, he was accused of attacking a Seal trainee and beating him almost to death. Realizing that he was involved in a great many things they would prefer not to have revealed in the course of a trial, the Navy discharged rather than prosecuted him. Then, well, he went private. Because he had previous experience with submersibles, that's where he gravitated to."

Gordon sighed as he settled back in his chair. "Three of my people have died. I trusted him. What am I going to tell Doctor Kline's wife?"

Standing on the mess deck surrounded by passengers and crew, Karen and Jason were finally surrendering to their exhaustion. There was nothing more they could do. Jason put his arm around her waist and she rested her head on his shoulder, no longer caring what anyone else on board might think of their feelings for each other.

"You saved my life, you know."

"Well," he responded, "I was only repaying you. It could have been me dead down there, days ago."

She smiled gently, stepped into him and placed her mouth on his as her arms surrounded his neck. After a deep kiss, she moved her lips an inch from his face and whispered: "Boy, do I wish we were anywhere else but on this ship!"

Jason only smiled stupidly and started to kiss her again.

THE END

~~~~~~~~~~~

WITH APPRECIATION

~~~~~~~~~~~~~~~~~~~~

Originally this book was to be a short story inspired by my own long-term engagement with the sea as a Navy officer, and my ongoing fascination with the deep ocean as presented in William J. Broad's marvelous book *The Universe Below*.

One thing led to another – ending in this novel in your hands. With a rough draft of *Deep Peril* in hand, I was lucky to gain rewrite and editorial help from my Princeton classmate John Selby, author of several dozen fiction and nonfiction books and screenplays. I'm deeply grateful to him and his partner Birgitta Steiner for all their guidance in helping me tighten and finish this novel, create the cover design, and gain a publisher.

Truly a team effort – many thanks!

www.ingramcontent.com/pod-product-compliance
Lightning Source LLC
Chambersburg PA
CBHW050426260626
47156CB00003B/1178